Gay Hunter

I care not if you bridge the seas
Or ride secure the cruel sky,
Or build consummate palaces
Of metal or of masonry,

But — have you wine and music still,
And statues, and a bright-eyed love?

JAMES ELROY FLECKER

Gay Hunter

J. Leslie Mitchell
(Lewis Grassic Gibbon)

With an introduction
'Lewis Grassic Gibbon and Science Fiction'
by Edwin Morgan

Polygon
EDINBURGH

© Polygon 1989

Introduction © Edwin Morgan 1989

First published in 1934
This edition first published in 1989 by
Polygon, 22 George Square, Edinburgh

Set in Berthold Sabon
by Hislop & Day, Edinburgh, and
printed and bound in Great Britain by
Redwood Burn Limited, Trowbridge, Wiltshire

British Library Cataloguing
  in Publication Data
Mitchell, J. Leslie (James Leslie, *1901-1935*)
Gay hunter,
I. Title
823'. 912 (F)

ISBN 0 7486 6049 6

The Publisher acknowledges subsidy from
the Scottish Arts Council towards the publication
of this volume.

CONTENTS

Lewis Grassic Gibbon and Science Fiction

GAY HUNTER affords a good example of trusting the tale rather than the teller. Gibbon wrote, in his dedication of the novel to Christopher Morley, that 'this book has no serious intent whatever' and that it was 'neither prophecy nor propaganda'. In fact, although the novel is a scientific romance, to use H. G. Wells' term, the romance element does not prevent it from being a perfectly serious and at times powerful book, nor is it devoid of either prophecy or propaganda. It is, as Gibbon himself said, a companion-piece to *Three Go Back* (1932). In the earlier novel, characters from the twentieth century travelling by airship across the Atlantic are wrecked on Atlantis and thrown back in time some 25,000 years, into the company of primitive but happy pre-agricultural hunters; in *Gay Hunter,* another trio of characters living in the south of England dreams itself forward some 20,000 years into a similar society of happy hunters, survivors in a post-apocalyptic world which has been ruined by atomic warfare. In both books the element of 'science' is a means to an end, but in *Gay Hunter* (which is much the better book) there is a genuine science-fiction interest, involving not only atomic bombs (a prophetic component in 1934) but also a laser-like lethal ray, seeing and listening devices akin to both television and radar, the use of unknown metals, and the altering of the constellations and of the position of sun and moon relative to the earth. Behind both books there is of course a whole science-fiction tradition, even at that date: backward time travel in Sir Arthur Conan Doyle's *The Lost World* (1912) and forward time travel in Wells's *The Time Machine* (1895) are two examples. Gibbon read much science-fiction, and although he turned violently against the progressivism of Wells he was clearly influenced by that writer, who is referred to in both *Three Go Back* and *Gay Hunter.* In *Gay Hunter* his heroine also mentions Bernard Shaw's epic drama *Back to Methuselah* (1918-1921), and although it is described as the 'eunuch's

i

dream' of a 'quack prophet' its ideas have obviously been pondered. Gay has read Aldous Huxley's *Brave New World* (1932) and clearly keeps up to date with science-fiction literature, despite what she calls the 'bleak lunacy' of Huxley's anthropological beliefs. And she does not forget one of the founding fathers of science-fiction, Camille Flammarion (1842-1925), the French astronomer, science popularizer, and writer of scientific romances such as *Omega: the Last Days of the World* (English translation, 1894).

The science-fiction element ought not perhaps to surprise us, since there are hints of it in many of Gibbon's books, even in *A Scots Quair* with its evoking of prehistoric memories, but more obviously in a work like *Hanno or the Future of Exploration* (1928), where a delighted and spirited sense of speculation informs and fleshes out an inquiry into the potential of man's urge to explore his submarine, subterranean, and finally extraterrestrial environment. For all Gibbon's mastery of local characteristics and recent history in *A Scots Quair*, there was always in his mind a desire to map out origins and futures, and his anthropological interests, taking him back into an ill-recorded or unrecorded past, could not but shade off into more imaginative constructs where belief rather than fact encouraged him to describe places and races, rituals and adventures, with a sort of didactic semi-fictionality, as in *The Conquest of the Maya* (1934), or in the full-blown fiction of his scientific romances.

Among the influences at work on *Gay Hunter*, made clear by Gibbon's frequent mention of it, is J. W. Dunne's *An Experiment with Time* (1928 and subsequent revised editions). This curious book, never wholly discredited but later neglected, made a strong impression, as I myself remember, throughout the 1930s, and was much discussed. Basically, it argued that the future as well as the past does actually exist, and that the dreaming mind of a sleeper is freed in both directions, so that precognition is possible. Dunne recommended that people should try to record dreams by writing them down as quickly as they could remember them; also that they should by various means encourage dreaming as an activity. The book must have seemed a godsend to Gibbon, who was thus presented with a (moderately) respectable scientific implement for unlocking future states. He uses it primarily as a device to get his characters into the future, but the theory also helped to suggest a certain continuity of the speculative mind, forwards as well as backwards, which suited his concern for sources and atavisms and extrapolations.

Another influence is the political situation of the early 1930s, and in particular the rise and spread of Fascism. The book is, among other things, a critique of Fascism. Of the three main characters, two are militant Fascists who disappear (probably destroyed) at the end of the book. Major Ledyard Houghton, with his barking voice, 'cold, aggressive eyes', and headaches resulting from poison gas tests during World War I, is an officer in the Fascist Defence Corps, and Lady Jane Easterling is the spoilt, bored, idle, cruel, haughty patron of the local Fascist group. These two near-caricatures are set in opposition to the heroine, Gay Hunter, who is more complex and is much more continuously at the forefront of the action. Perhaps because she is a young American archeologist, visiting England to attend a conference, she is allowed to be a more detached and more democratic observer. It is she who does everything in her power to thwart the establishment of a Fascist-type colony by Houghton and Lady Jane in the ruined future London where the action converges. Yet it is not, and could hardly be at the date when it was written, a straightforward anti-Fascist parable. The authoritarian and irascible Major is nevertheless the one who helps Gay to escape after she has been taken prisoner and tied to a pillar to await execution by giant rats. And Gay herself does not invariably condemn Houghton and his kind. After her release she is as determined as ever that the two Fascists must be killed, despite Houghton's having taken temporary pity on her, but she is willing to see them as victims of society, and not merely as evil activists:

Yet — were even they to blame? They were no more than victims of their one-time environment and education and social caste; and the aberrant culture that companioned that caste in the days of its economic straits.   (p. 161)

iii

The wider political concerns of the book relate to Fascism but go beyond it. The long-dead Hierarchs, whose ruined civilization litters the venue where the action climaxes, but whose story is told through the recorded Voices that Gay switches on, ruled like super-Fascists in huge socially polarized War States which preyed on one another and subsisted on the labour of a slave class of eugenically controlled Sub-Men. Disaster overtook them when a last desperate rebellion of Sub-Men coincided with an unparalleled outbreak of atomic war between the Hierarchies. Despite Gay's horror as she listens to the story of 'the Sub-Men, the Ancient Lowly', Gibbon allows us to hear how the voice of this hubris-rich civilization, knowing itself to be doomed, would defend itself:

> ' . . . in comparison with them [the Hierarchies] the greatest achievements of the earliest scientific age of the old Christ-age superstition are little more than the fumblings of savages in the dark. We have measured the stars and sent ships to the planets, we have prolonged life and mitigated death, created new life in the test-tubes of our laboratories, altered the periodicity of the seasons, reached in the arts the verge of a world that definitely marks a new and subtle transformation of the human mind. But now it seems that all this glorious fabric may be either completely or partially levelled in the Revolt of the Sub-Men . . . ' (p. 86)

This Baconian dream of science, not unshared by Gibbon at certain moments, as his book *Hanno* makes clear, and by no means incomprehensible to the heroine, who after all has had a scientific training, is nevertheless shown to be morally corrupt in its hand-in-glove association with totalitarian régimes. Gibbon attempts, unsuccessfully, to categorize the moral corruption by vaguely worded references to some unspeakable 'filth' in the Hierarchs' 'Testament of Life', with which the voice ends. Sufficient muscle is given to the main body of the Hierarchs' self-defence to dramatize a meaningful opposition to them, the key loophole in their argument being their scornful mention of 'the fumblings of savages in the dark'. This thoughtlessly uttered comparison, used merely to dismiss twentieth-century achievements, introduces what to both Gay Hunter and Gibbon is not a negative but an enormous positive.

The central theme of the book, brought out through the peregrinations and encounters of the heroine as she adjusts to, and is liberated by, the primitive society of nomad hunters she meets in post-Armageddon England, will be familiar to readers of Gibbon: before civilization delivered its discontents, there was a Golden Age of free-range human life, unorganized but kindly, ignorant of deceit and depravity, unwarlike and co-operative; what *Gay Hunter* adds, by way of perspective, is that once civilization, in an orgy of self-destruction, has vanished, that Golden Age can still return, among the survivors, and (because it is, in a sense, the second time round, a second chance for human experience) can even hold out a mysteriously undefined potential for development which will not be 'civilization' in the bad old sense. This development, if it should occur, would perhaps relate to a certain dialectic the story has been presenting between Gay's physical, sensuous liberation and her occasional and very natural outbursts of impatience with the simple life. Sitting watching the sun set one evening, she suddenly sees in her memory, 'as though torn from a kinematographic reel', the faces and lights and buildings of Broadway and the Strand, and feels an intense longing for the multiplex life she has lost:

> She might live for fifty or sixty years yet — *how?* Roaming the countryside with a wolf, eating fruit, climbing trees — she would go mad! Life an eternal picnic — it was the kind of thing that sick little imaginative novelists had dreamt of in the smoke and squalor and the unemployment queues of the fourth decade of the twentieth century. (p. 59)

How much self-rebuke there is in this, on Gibbon's part, is hard to say, but it certainly helps the drama of the story. The attitude of Major Houghton to the society of the Folk could be guessed from what he said before he left the twentieth

v

century. He looked forward to seeing less 'modernist botching' and more 'discipline and breed and good taste', and when Gay asks him sceptically if that really is the future, he replies: 'Of course it is. Service, loyalty. Hardness. Hierarchy. The scum in their places again.' Once he gets to know the Folk, he itches to have them organised, drilled, armed, and of course commanded by himself and an eventual élite of oligarchs. His first practical step, however, is to give formal expression to his outraged moral decencies: he and Lady Jane make themselves grass kilts to dissociate their state from the universal nakedness. There are therefore three factors to the equation: the Folk with a threatened disruption of their settled life, the two Fascists searching for opportunities to exert their sway, and Gay herself, revelling in her new freedom yet twitching now and again under its undemanding emptiness.

The drama of the book is kept at a relatively rudimentary level, since crucial actions are somewhat thinly spread out, but the story had considerable narrative and evocative power, both on the level of following an adventure and more particularly in its use of suspense, in the constant mentioning of London before that city is reached. Nor does the vision of London, when we finally see it (Book 2, Chapter 5, 'The Ruins'), disappoint. References to Gustave Doré's engravings and James (B.V.) Thomson's *The City of Dreadful Night* are misleading until we take them in conjunction with the fact that it was known to the Folk as the Shining Place; it was a ruin, but the gigantic buildings, only partly damaged, though wholly deserted by the long-dead builders, were not of masonry but of a rustless, indestructible metal — a mile-high phallic pillar still intact, a jagged terraced ziggurat where St Paul's Cathedral had once been, a high blue surveillance disc still working and revolving. The headily suggestive mix of Indian lingam-worship, Aztec sacrifice, and advanced technology, in a place now home to rats and bats, is truly remarkable, and is itself a cunning comment on an earlier interior monologue by Gay, soon after meeting the Folk, where she tries to digest the new situation: 'The England of Shakespeare, Newton, Avebury — it had ended in nakedness, brown skins, and a bow...' Culture, science, and an ancient sacred site — but she did not know yet that their transformed selves had not really 'ended' but were still in the frightening, towering, half-functioning presences of the Shining Place. And this she had to see — 'Lovely, fantastic and terrible London!' — before its final fiery annihilation.

> It rose gigantic in the afternoon air, perhaps five miles away, a great waste of tumbled pylons that caught the sunlight dazzlingly from cliffs and precipices of unrusting metal and flung that sheen high and blindingly into the air. At first the shapes of the great buildings seemed to move and change before her eyes, then the last of the mist rolled down into the place where the sea came, and she saw the London of the Hierarchs, as they had left it thousands of years before, when the plagues came and the Sub-Men rose. (p. 147)

But underlying these large themes is the book's continuing romance, its idyll of rustic love, the tentatively developed but then intensely sensual affair between virginal American archeologist Gay and downy-bearded rippling-muscled young hunter and singer Rem. The first time his hand touched her arm, it 'felt as though an electric dynamo were stroking her.' All through the book, the much-repeated word 'naked' never lets us forget that Gay and Rem are totally unclothed, as are all the Folk, whatever they may be doing, and that this nakedness (which has odd quasi-Fascist resonances from the German cult of the nude body in the 'twenties and 'thirties, culminating in Leni Riefenstahl's famous Olympic film) symbolizes the candour and innocence of their relationship in a way that needs no sanctification from priest or church. There are awkwardnesses in Gibbon's presentation of Gay's character, and of her way of speaking; English dialogue was never his strong point. It says something for the force of the narrative that the potential embarrassments which seem to come thick and fast in the early chapters simply fall away as the novel gathers momentum. Even the return to familiar England at the end, when she is found after six years, still naked, in a clover meadow, and is fussed over by Nurse Geddes and offered gruel, manages — just — to conquer its own bathos and show her resilience of character. 'I'm not mad, and I'm not ill, but I've been twenty thousand years away. And I haven't come back for gruel.' Right!

Edwin Morgan.

For

Christopher Morley

Dear Christopher Morley,

This is not, in any sense, a sequel to 'Three Go Back'. But I suppose it might be called a companion book; and I hope Gay in the forests of futurity will please your lighter hours as much as Clair did when we three hunted aurochsen on the plains of pre-history.

My main work is to pry in the ruins of your own incomparable continent, and I wrote 'Gay Hunter' in the pauses of writing a history of the Maya. But though I found my theme in those solemnities of research and sent it to hunt a new home in space and time, this book has no serious intent whatever. (The star-chaos of that distant night-time sky is, I'm well aware, unlikely.) It is neither prophecy nor propaganda. It is written for the glory of sun and wind and rain, dreams by smoking camp-fires, and the glimpsed immortality of men.

(Still, though the Hierarchs may never happen, I have a wistful hope for the Hunters!)

Sincerely,
J. Leslie Mitchell.

1934

BOOK I

GAY GO UP

1. The Compact

i

GAY HUNTER stood in the blow of the wind on the Wiltshire Downs and surveyed the landscape with a drowsy approval.

Below and around her, and curving in long lines of pastelled background, the unfamiliar moors quivered and moved their cloaks in the coming of the afternoon wind. Rightwards and downwards she could see the pillared ruins of Stonehenge: Pewsey slept amidst its trees, Netheravon edged the skyline with its barracks, far on the flagstaffs of Upavon the wind indicator bellied in the breeze over the aerodrome lost in the grasses below. Gay found it very peaceful. She liked the change of peace. It was hard to believe it England or, indeed, her century in any land at all. If the barracks and wind indicators were to vanish, leaving the landscape to the curlews and herself, she might half believe it the world of the antique men....

'Still thinking shop,' she reproved herself, drowsily.

She found great amusement in reproving herself. For, on the whole, she rather approved than disapproved of this self that lived and looked and ate and dreamed and slept and worked and had a passion for temple-measurement and an acute distaste for the English method of cooking cabbages; and puzzled a bright, enquiring gaze at Alpha in Centaur at night; and liked to sleep without sheets, between blankets, because it tickled one amusingly; and loathed trains, trench-mortars, and all the American Presidents but two; and bore with glad fools gladly, being, she recognised, something in the same category; and thought of dying and going out of sight of the sun as a sad thing, not the matter for indifference or passionate hope that others thought it; and intended to have two babies sometime — not all at once, twins would

3

be a trial, in a space of three years better; and wondered how it would feel to sleep with a man — rather silly and fun, perhaps; and liked hard chocolates best, because she had good teeth — funny teeth, they met and bit edge to edge as the teeth of the Cro-Magnard men did; and liked lying in bed with her heels on the bed-rail, reading poetry by Gertrude Stein, and giggling; and liked to walk in rain, with the sting in her face, and come back, and strip, and shiver like a cat — lovely that shiver that shook one's skin clear of one's bones for a second; and approved her own bones, though they *were* rather on the large side. . . .

'What a category!' She sighed and laughed and sat down on the hill-brow. There was a little pool below. She lighted a cigarette and put back her hair from her forehead, and considered herself for a while, blowing away the wreathings of smoke that she might see herself better. The crouched image surveyed her with nice cool eyes that had a golden twinkle in them: something peculiar in the pigmentation of her eyes, her father had told her — they glowed, faintly, cat-like in the dark. Peculiar enough, for they were a deep, dark blue. She had nostrils that lifted and fell a little while she slept or breathed deeply or smiled — they did so now. Oh yes, and she could waggle her ears. She did so now.

Five feet eight inches in height, though that wasn't very observable in this attitude, and a passable figure — in Greek fashion, not the Chino-battered-Perso-corseteered figure of the moderns. You couldn't have that kind of figure with bones rather big and archaic, like your teeth. . . . She could see the brown detritus at the bottom of the pool, and, leaning forward so, the collar of her green dress that flapped forward to frame her head and face, prettily, she thought, though immodestly, for she could look down on the dress of her reflection to a gleam and shadow of shapely breasts. They tilted a little, not white, but brown. That came of the sun-bathing in Mexico.

A peewit flapped overhead. Gay raised her head and looked at it, and forgot her reflection and her drowse of thoughts. Very readily in such surroundings she could forget herself and her times. She lowered her eyes from the curlew-haunted, wind-haunted wastes of the Downs to

4

the fringement of terraces under her feet. In ancient times the prospectors from across the seas had been here. Here they had built their terraced fields up into the blow of even such winds as blew upon her now. And before their time, here in the world's spring, the hunters had hunted free and naked through forest and bush, with no dream of that which awaited their kind in the deeps of the future. So long ago, so long ago! It was a fairy-tale and yet a fact that a little American girl sat on the Wiltshire Downs and looked back upon, remote from her world and even her work, yet with a note like an ancient music sounding undying even in these times. . . .

These times: Gay looked back over her twenty-three years of life, to crowded cities and desolate countryside, to her years of reading and hearing and debating, to her three weeks here in England. Civilisation: this for which men had sold their birthright; this which they were so anxious to preserve!

She glanced at the sun. It had smouldered down low over the indicators on the far-off aerodrome. She must get back.

ii

She had parked the hired Morgan from London a little way off the road. Getting into it, she threw away her cigarette and concentrated on the unfamiliar gears, with their unfamiliar feel. A sudden revulsion against the Downs had come upon her. She'd go back to Pewsey and have tea and lie on her bed and read up those notes on pottery periodicity in the Toltec pueblos.

The road was deserted, fringed by long grasses, dry and rustling. Sheep baaed far off and unseen. Presently Gay was aware that the road was no longer deserted. She had overtaken a man who seemed to be in distress. He was squatting by the side of the road, his head in his hands. His brown hair was greying a bit, she noted, absently, as she stopped the Morgan and got out of it, lithely, even though her figure was so pleasingly unmodern. The man raised his head.

'Well?'

5

Gay said, 'I thought you were ill.'

'I'm not.'

'Sorry.'

She went back to the Morgan, wriggled into it, and was just pressing the self-starter when she heard him call to her. 'Can you give me a ride to Pewsey?'

'Plenty of room,' Gay remarked.

He got up then and approached. He was tall. He might have been forty years of age, she thought, from his skin at the neck, round and clean. But his face was older — set with lines of unhappy years, with beetling brows and unhappy, cold, aggressive eyes. He was in hiker's kit — shirt and shorts and rucksack. She noted he had small feet. (You could not help noting things like that when someone else sat beside you in a Morgan.) He disposed them into as small a place as possible.

'Okay?' she asked.

'I'm all right.... Oh, hell!'

His hands flew up to his forehead, gripping it. Gay took her hands from the self-starter. She was a little startled, but not too much. In her handbag was a bottle of aspirins. She fetched it out.

'Try some of these.'

He took his hands from his eyes and looked at the aspirins and then at her; and was suddenly, violently and blasphemously obscene.

'.... blasted muck ... ride in your confounded bath-tub, not your opinion of my ailments. Haven't I had enough of the half-witted doctors and their cures without you trying to poison me? Blasted rubbish....'

Gay lighted a fresh cigarette, reflecting absently that she smoked too much. 'What's the funny badge on your shirt?'

'Eh?'

They both surveyed the badge. It was in blue and green enamel, a bundle of rods and an axe tied round with thongs. The curlews called. The wind had quietened away, awaiting the going down of the sun. The man scowled.

'The fasces.'

Gay, starting the Morgan at last, said that she saw that. And what did the fasces stand for?

'The Fascists.'

6

'I see.' For a little Gay was polite and absent, doing active things round a hair-pin bend. 'Then you're a Fascist?'

He grunted. Gay was faintly amused. Then, suddenly she remembered the story told her by one of the German delegates at the Americanist Congress — of his sister, a communist, who had had her . . . . She felt sick even now to remember it. And this freak with the headache and the hiker's shirt was of the party that had been pleased to do *that*. Gay stopped the Morgan with a shriek of brakes. She was still polite.

'Sorry I made a mistake. Will you get out?'

The man stared, his lips parting slightly. He had pleasant teeth. He said, 'Eh?'

'Get out. I like to help people' — she tried to speak lightly and indifferently, but the story of what had happened to that German woman kept wheeling the ordure of its details around the mind, and she felt that in a moment she would vomit — 'but I really draw the line at people like . . . . We won't bother to debate it. Will you get out?'

His lined face flushed deeply. 'Too pleased,' he said. In moments of stress his intonation was Oxford. Gay retorted in a burlesque Cambridge.

'*So nice.*'

But the Morgan is a small machine. His legs had become tangled in Gay's raincoat, lying at the bottom of the car. He tugged with one foot, then another, bent down, swore. Gay had a desire to giggle, her anger fading. Suddenly he desisted from his efforts, his hands flying up to his head again. . . . A minute later Gay was saying:

'You poor man, I was a beast. Lean back here, and you'll be comfy. I'll run you into Pewsey and we'll dig out a doctor. You look bad.'

The intermittent attack of pain had passed. He hesitated a moment. His voice had lost its previous roughness.

'Thank you. Afraid I behaved like a lout. But these infernal pains . . . .'

'Ophthalmia?' Gay was coasting along in low gear.

'Something like that to begin with. My eyes are all right, but I had a whiff of a test gas towards the end of the war that upset a balance somewhere. Only these headaches have

7

grown worse in the last three months.' He winced again. 'And I can't sleep —I tell you I can't.... Sorry.'

'No need to be. Must feel terrible. But surely they've given you sleeping draughts?'

He sneered. '*And* imaginary sheep to count.'

Gay gave it up. After a little she knew he was glancing at her. He said: 'You're an American, aren't you?'

'Gay Hunter, archaeologist. Father American, mother English. Born Mexico City. Education: none. Age: twenty-three. Father and mother dead. Business in England: attending Americanist Congress.'

He drawled: 'Don't bother with your size in shoes and your taste in underwear. I'm Major Ledyard Houghton. Retired from Army with intermittent ill-health a year ago. Half-pay. An officer in the Fascist Defence Corps. Father and mother dead.'

'The meeting of the orphans, in fact,' said Gay. 'Any particular place you want to go to in Pewsey?'

'There was a sort of hotel there — the "Peacock"— I noticed passing through this morning. I could get a bed there, I think.'

'Sure to.' Gay agreed. 'It's where I'm staying and there seem to be plenty of empty rooms.'

'Very good of you to take along anything so repulsive as a Fascist.'

'Yet, it is rather. But I suppose they're not to blame — in origin, anyhow. Bad anthropology and worse history, and the lunatic blitherings of Sigmund Freud are responsible, not the funny little Mosleys or Hitlers or Mussolinis ... Yes?'

His eyebrows were fluttering again. His politeness had quite gone. 'Your history's on a par with your accent.'

Gay was maddeningly complacent. 'A very good accent. Elizabethan, we Americans talk, you know. ... Well, here's Pewsey.'

iii

She abandoned him at the hotel entrance and went and stabled the Morgan. The weather still held; it was

8

stiflingly hot in her bedroom, with the ivy tapping against the window in the hot little breeze. Gay took off her clothes and fanned herself with some sheets of the report on Toltec pottery, the while she read some of the others. Then she rang for tea, and draped herself with the sheets when the girl brought it up. The girl smiled, liking Gay. Most people liked her, wistfully. There came a thump of heavy boots entering the next room. Gay raised enquiring brows.

'Let that room at last, Miss,' the girl confided. 'Queer-looking gentleman.'

Gay stretched her toes and disembarrassed herself of the Toltec report. 'Mind if I disrobe? I thought it might be the waiter, and I'd hate to embarrass the poor man.'

'He'd have enjoyed it all right, Miss.'

Gay nodded. (She was funny, but nice, the girl decided.) 'Suppose he might. And I wouldn't. What a wind we all want to blow away the cobwebs! . . . Let next door, did you say?'

'Yes, Miss. Funny gentleman who can't sleep, I heard him telling the master.'

Gay recognised the description. 'Well, he won't keep me awake with snores. Tray here, yes. Thanks.'

By the time the darkness had rendered reading out of the question, she had nearly finished the report. She lay on the bed and looked at herself; then whistled a little. Tomorrow she would be finished with this Wiltshire glimpse, and go back to London by way of Nurse Geddes' cottage at Pinner, before she sailed for America. Dear, pleasant, plump, admonitory Nurse Geddes! — who had loved and tended and smacked her early days into shape in Mexico after Mother died, and now, pensioned and retired, grew flowers, poultry, and a schoolgirl complexion in a cottage that had for happy adjuncts a large, lovely and quite useless clover meadow and a night-view of London upon the sky . . . . It was Nurse Geddes who had taught her that old rhyming play on her name, she remembered:

> 'Gay go up, and Gay go down:
> That is the way to London Town!'

She twisted around on the bed. London? Nurse was

welcome to it — and every other big town in fact or fancy. Though one sometimes had a moment's passionate desire for New York, its lights, a good theatre's entertainment, a flaring headline on a *real* news-sheet. . . .

Only they had begun to haunt her these days, newspapers. (Delayed adolescence, she supposed.) Idiotic to let them do that and spoil her holiday after all that work at the Americanist Congress. Idiotic — but the stuff of them had begun to spoil her lightest moments, with their dreary listings of tariffs and bickerings, strikes and hunger-marches, mounted police charges on London's unemployed, the drowsy mummings of the English parliament, the growing poverty and cumulating horror of a civilisation in the agonies of every civilisation's internal contradictions. War and the rumours of war again, blowing up smokily from the four corners of the world. Hunger and murder and famine coming on seven-league boots, the beasts and savages of civilisation gathering under the swastika flag. . . .

Like Houghton. She shivered. Good thing it had been no more than a road encounter. Something about him as repulsive as about an unwashed baby — more, babies didn't know and couldn't help it, and *did* enjoy a bath so much once you held them firmly and scrubbed hard, and twinkled coloured bubbles in front of them — kicked and laughed and enjoyed being clean and having lovely skins. (She'd washed babies in Mexico.) But from Houghton and his kind you couldn't wash off the foul beliefs and superstitions that came out of the dreary past and equipped them with knives wherewith to cut the throats of all the decent traits in civilisation. . . .

'If you *can* cut the throat of a trait . . . my dear, you want your dinner.'

She dressed for it in no more than a vest, step-ins, and the thinner of her two frocks, found shoes for her bare feet, and went down to the dining-room. The air was even more stifling here, though the windows were wide open. A gramophone was playing somewhere in Pewsey — playing a song nearly as out of date as the Pewsey statues, in the slobbery Oxford-cum-Cambridge accent in which English lyrics are sung:

10

'Gaw-id sendew bahk . . . toomee,
Oh-ver thah mitey seee . . .

       .   .   .

Daily I wanchew, Oh, how I mishew . . .'

Oh, slop, slop, slop! What a poor wail out of the dark and terror and stench and filth of those war-time years that she herself had never known. . . . Mexico then, bright with tamarinds and bandits and the sun: while the starved and scared women in cinemas were weeping over that tosh, and going home to lonely beds in the fug of just such rooms as this. Poor things, poor things. What was Mother's English adjectival phrase?: 'Too bloody.' Worse than that. (Gay, my dear, have a big dinner and get back to the Toltecs and their pottery.)

She looked round the room and its sham antique oak, all solemn lines of fiddley curlicues. A great sloped mirror showed herself. Being still very young, she looked at that self with attention, but not too much. The room was deserted but for the waiter bringing the soup. Then she saw Houghton enter.

He had changed from hiking-dress — perhaps he had carried that lounge suit in the rucksack. It certainly looked a trifle crumpled. And as certainly it improved his appearance. Gay drank soup and looked at him with a faint interest — he had good shoulders and a straight back, and the cool hauteur and rangy straightness of the English Army officer of myth and rumour. As good almost as meeting an ancient Mayan in the flesh.

Funny how much better the lounge suit was than the hiking-shirt and shorts. But she'd thought that often of the feeble attempts at rationalisation in clothes that men and women made. The scantier the garments, the more feeble and ridiculous and lewd the wearers looked. The Victorians were perfectly right and logical, bless their padded bottoms. Either you clothed yourself or you went naked. To sling shorts or the various pieces of a bathing suit over this and that portion of your anatomy was to make those portions suspect and taboo. . . .

Houghton was standing beside her. He was stiff. 'I

understand the waiter would like us to share a table and save him work. Lazy old devil. Do you mind?'

Gay shook her head, eating tepid fish. 'I don't think so.' She turned away her eyes from another fasces badge, in the lapel of the lounge suit collar this time. 'How's the headache?'

He sat down, half in profile. It was a stern, good, absurd profile. 'Gone for the time being; but no doubt it'll come back.... No, damn you, I told you I didn't want soup. A chop, man.'

This was to the waiter. He shook a little, old and servile. Gay gently restrained herself from flinging the remains of the tepid fish at the correct, absurd profile. She had often to restrain herself over bodily assault in matters like that. The damned horror of any animal addressing another like that! Then she saw the twist of Houghton's face. Poor idiot.

She said: 'There's a stunt in sleep-making that my father and I used to use when we went digging down in Central America. Ever hear of a man J. W. Dunne?'

'Eh? ... No.'

'He's not a quack doctor or a psychoanalyst. He wrote a book called *An Experiment with Time*, and Father got hold of it. If you develop the trick you can get to sleep quite easily — unless you grow too interested in tomorrow morning.'

'Oh.'

But Gay was not discouraged. It was two or three years since she herself had tried those experiments at the edge of sleeping to peer into the doings of the next day or so. Father had given it up. He had said it was dangerous without elaborate precautions — funny father, the sternest and best of materialists! — salt of the earth, the materialists, though there *was* all this half-witted outcry against them these days from the sloppily superstitious Quakers who masqueraded as physicists.... Well, this was how....

The old waiter sighed, peering round the edge of the door. That young 'un from America was at it with the gentleman. Bit sharp, the gentleman, but you supposed he couldn't be blamed. You were getting old, and a bit deaf, though it made you run cold to think of that, and that the boss would get to know.... He looked again. Still at it, she was.

Houghton said, 'Sounds rubbish. How can you look into the future — into a time that doesn't exist?'

Gay shrugged. She was a little bored herself, by now. This bleak militaristic intelligence always bored her — made flirting with ship officers and gendarmes impossible. Kind of people who never thought of the thrill of a kiss as the moment before lips touched, but just the contact and crush and a greedy suction.... 'The point seems to be that events don't happen. They're waiting there in the future to be overtaken.'

He said 'Rubbish,' again grumpily; then jabbed at his chop and was suddenly loquacious.

'By God, there would be something worth while if one *could* have a glimpse of the future — project oneself into it for no more than a blink. All this modernist botching of society and art and civilisation finished, and discipline and breed and good taste come into their own again. Worth while trying half a night of sleeplessness to see that.'

Gay had been about to rise and have her coffee on the verandah; but now she could not, looking at him with bent brows.

'Is that what the future is to be?'

'Of course it is. Service, loyalty. Hardness. Hierarchy. The scum in their places again.' His face twitched. 'England a nation again.'

'And beyond that?'

'What would there be? Some dignity in history; the national cultures keeping the balance....'

Gay whistled. 'Poor human race! Is that its future? Well, whatever's awaiting it, I know it isn't that.'

'Some Amurrican Utopia instead, with every nation denationalised and the blah of your accent all over the globe?'

'That's just rudeness.'

He coloured, stiffly. 'I'm sorry.'

Gay said: 'Even tomorrow won't show a glimpse of anything as bad as that. Or beyond it. If we sat down tonight and tried to glimpse the future, we'd find most things we expect haven't happened....'

'All right. Let's put it to the test tonight, according to the formula of this chap Dunne that your father developed.

13

Lie and try a glimpse into the future — and see if it's your Utopia or a sane history that the future's going to hold.'

Gay said: 'Of course that's just fantastic. You can see only a little of your own future — through a glass darkly.'

He was holding his head again. He was really ill, Gay thought. He said, with the rudeness of pain and unease: 'Afraid, like most softies, eh?'

Gay knew it was silly, but also the project was a little intriguing. She shrugged. 'All right. Let's. But — if we manage to see anything at all — how are we to know when we compare results that each is speaking the truth?'

'I'm not a liar.'

Gay nodded, rising. 'Lucky man. Well, I'll be seeing you.'

iv

The heat grew more stifling as the night wore on. Ascending to her room at eleven, Gay found the warmth swathing the place like a thick close blanket. 'Like Coleridge's pants, in fact.' Coleridge provided one of her gayest memories:

'As though the earth in thick fast pants
were breathing.'

'Poor planet, how it must have perspired! And I feel a bit like it myself.'

She took off her dress and step-ins and kicked off her shoes and sat with her hands clasping her brown knees, and looked out at the hot, stagnant night of the Wiltshire Downs. Below, she heard the old waiter closing up for the night, and the sound of heavy footsteps enter the room next her own. She thought: 'The haughty Britisher with the headaches,' and sat remembering their pact. The foolishest thing — especially as she didn't feel in the least in the mood for trying a neo-Dunne test to-night. . . . She picked up the newspaper she had brought unread from the smoking-room and opened it and began to read. The night went on. At midnight she heard

14

the clocks chime below, and woke to the lateness of the hour with a little start:

What a world! Hell 'n' blast, what a world! — as Daddy used to say in moments when it vexed him overmuch. The cruelty, the beastliness, the hopelessness of it. Not for herself — she stretched brown and clean, and looked down at herself and liked herself and thought of her lovely job among the remains of the Antique Americans and her plan for a couple of babies, not to mention a father for them, and for reading a million books and seeing a million sunrises. But she was only one, and a fortunate one.... All the poor folk labouring at filthy jobs under the gathering clouds of war and an undreamed tyranny — what *had* they to live for? Even she herself — would she always escape? Unless she hid from her kind in the busy world of men, sought out some little corner and abandoned life like the folk at Rainier, like the hermits of the Thebaid. Those children of hers — would they escape the wheels and wires of life any more than the children of others? Or their children thereafter, and so on and on, till the world was one great pounding machine, pounding the life out of humanity, making it an ant-like slave-crawl on an earth turned to a dung-hill of its own futilities. She thought of Houghton next door — he was more than Houghton, he was the brutalised and bedevilled spirit of all men, she thought. And for them and their horrific future they expected women to conceive and have fruitful bodies and bear children....

Suddenly the night outside seemed to crack. Sheet lightning flowed low and saffron down over Pewsey, lighting up the Downs, and flowing soft in the foliage of the trees. Gay went to the window and watched. The earth looked a moment like a sea of fire, as though that Next War's bombardments were opening their barrage. It was hotter than ever.

She got into her sleeping-suit, put out the light, and lay down with only a sheet covering her. So doing, the view of the night vanished, for the windows were high in the wall. She stretched her toes and put her right arm under her head in the fashion that always so helped her to sleep, and closed her eyes.

15

Half an hour later she had tried most positions conceivable and inconceivable. But the newspapers were haunting her from sleep. She got up and drank a glass of water — tepid water that seemed to have dust in it. Low down over Upavon the thunder was growling dyspeptically. She lay down again, throwing off the sheet this time, and lay open-eyed, staring into the darkness, young, and absurdly troubled, she told herself, a little whipper-snapper absurdly and impudently troubled over a planet that wasn't her concern.... Except that she hated the thought of those babies of hers, in the times to be, coughing and coughing up their lungs as the war-gas got into them....

It was only then that she remembered again her pact with the Fascist, Houghton.

v

Dreams, and a floating edge of mist. (But you must not dream. You must stay just on the edge of sleep, concentrating. So that you might awake and jot down your impressions of the pictures.) She tried to rouse herself, but a leaden weight seemed pressing now on her eyelids. Yet again she told herself not to dream.

Outside the lightning flashed, forked lightning as she knew through her closed eyelids. But now the dream-pictures were mist-edged no longer, they were jagged like the lightning. She knew herself caught in a sudden flow of images she had never tapped before — slipping and sliding amidst them like a diver going over Niagara. Something suddenly snapped and the pictures ceased....

Bombardment. The sky burst and showered the earth with glowing meteors. Great-engined monsters roared athwart the earth. Tribes fled and hid in dim confusion and climbed out again to the burning day. Great temples rose to insane creeds, and gangs of red dwarfs laboured at titanic furnaces. Peace flowed and flowered with winking seasons, season on season. Then again the sky broke and flared with terror. Now faster and faster went her fall over and into an unthinkable

16

abyss, in a wink and flow of green and gold and jet. Ceaseless and ceaseless.

Then something smote athwart the rapids, and the pit opened and devoured her.

2. The Incredible Morning

i

SHE OPENED her eyes and saw that it was not yet dawn. There was a pale light all abroad the great stretches of the Wiltshire Downs, forerunner of the sunlight, but only a ghost of its quality. A little rain was seeping away into the east. She heard the patter of its going, light-footed, through the darkness into the spaces where the east was wanly tinted. She sat up.

Close at hand a curlew called.

She was aware that she was still dreaming, for the window of the room in the 'Peacock' was set high in the wall, so that, lying in bed, as she lay now, she could see nothing of Pewsey or the Downs beyond. This was a fragment of night-time dream. Drowsy, she lay back again, cuddling her face in her arm, and reaching out her left hand to draw up the sheets about her. Her fingers strayed uncertainly, finding no sheet. With a sleepy irritation she sought further, and then sat up again. There was no sheet. But something else had led her to sit erect. Her hand had touched her own skin.

She was naked.

She put out her hand in the dimness and touched the bed. It was not a bed. She was lying on a bank of earth — a grassy bank. It was wet with dew. Her back and legs were wet and chilled with the dew. She sat erect, very rigid, her hands behind her.

The curlew called again, very close at hand. Wings flapped in the dimness, darkness-shielded, and there came a splatter of something in a hidden pool. Gay put up her hand to her mouth and bit it.

She gave a cry at the realness of the pain. What was it? Where. . . . ?

Hell 'n' blast, she knew! Sleep-walking! Not that she

18

had ever sleep-walked before, that she knew. But that was what it must be. She had got out of her room and out of the 'Peacock,' and wandered out to the country beyond Pewsey. What a mess!

She rubbed her chilled self and put up a hand to push back the hair from her forehead. Soon be quite light — probably not yet four o'clock. She must get back. With a little luck she might get back unseen. The labourers' wives would just be stirring to light their morning fires.

She stood erect; and instantly sat down, gasping. There was something strange in the morning air that caught at her lungs, icily as though she had swallowed a mouthful of snow. Now she became aware of another fact — the rate at which her heart was beating. It was pounding inside her chest, insanely, and the blood throbbing in her forehead with the rapid beat of a dynamo. Sleep-walking and nightmare — Oh, what a fool!

She sat with her head in her hands, giddy, till the world about her began to quiet into unquivering outlines. Her heart was easing to normal pulsations. Through her fingers she saw the dawn coming on Pewsey.

And there was no Pewsey.

ii

She sat in a great dip of the Downs, grassy and treeless, houseless, without moving speck of life, that she could see, north, south, east or west. In the coming of the sun great hummocks at a distance shed themselves of shadows, they seemed like great tumuli as the light came upon them. A wind was coming with the light, and blew cold with dew. But it changed and grew warmer, blowing upon her naked body, blowing her hair about her face. Below the little incline on which she sat a stream that wandered through the great hollow in the Downs lost itself in a reed-fringed stretch of water: she saw that it was a marsh-fringed loch, stretching its reeds away to the foot of the tumuli.

She began to weep, terrified and lost, watching that

19

bright becoming of the day. Hell 'n' blast, she was mad — mad, or in a nightmare still. Where was her room and her clothes and that report on Toltec pottery?

She closed her eyes, sticking them fast, gripping her head in her hands. Then she dropped them and opened her eyes. She gave a low cry.

A great beast had come snuffling up the hill from the reeds and stood not a yard away from her, gigantic in the half-light, with pricked ears and a drooling tongue. Its musk smell smote her like a blow. It had the bigness of a bear, though the shape of a wolf. It gave a low wurr and dropped one ear.

Gay screamed, piercingly.

At that the beast backed away, growled blood-curdlingly, then turned, clumsily, and trotted away. Gay watched it with a breathless disbelief as it entered the reeds. A grunt and yap emerged. The reeds ceased to wave and move. Gay's frozen silence went.

'Lost, lost — oh, I'm lost!' She screamed the words, knowing that someone would come and shake her awake and help her — that chambermaid, perhaps. She stared about her wide-eyed, waiting that coming. The day brightened and grew.

No smoke. No sign of a house or of human habitation. She raised her eyes to the east and saw against it a moving dot. It grew and enlarged, coming earthwards and nearer. She held her breath.

It was a great bird the size of a condor, and something of the same shape, with a crooked beak and immense pinions that beat the air with the noise of a river paddle-boat. It might have been twelve feet from wing-tip to wing-tip. It planed down close to the earth, to the spot where Gay stood and glared, uttered a raucous and contemptuous 'Arrh,' and wheeled up into the sky again.

A condor *in England!*

Gay began to talk to herself. At the first word the silence of the deserted countryside seemed to intensify, listening. Breathtaking and terrible.

'I don't care! This isn't real, but I won't go mad! I won't, I ...'

She realised she was dreadfully thirsty, her lips grimed as with ancient dust. She glanced down at her body and saw it the same, covered evenly as with a thin sprinkling of soot. With a desperate courage she looked towards the loch. The beast . . . ?

She picked up a stone in each hand and ran down into the water. It caught her and almost choked her, deep. She dropped the stones and splashed and swam, gasping. Something in the water caught at a foot, slimily, but she kicked it away. When she swam back to the shore again and climbed, gasping, from the icy embrace of the water, and wrung that water from her hair and wiped it from breasts and body and legs, she felt as though she had sloughed more than the covering of brown soot-dust. Wiping the water from her eyelashes, she raised her head again, knowing that surely the icy dip would have restored her sanity as it had cleansed her body. Around her were the unfamiliar, treeless, uninhabited hills. Then she saw something white rising up from the foot of the incline where she herself had awakened. It elongated and stretched, cruciform-wise. It was suddenly rigid. It was a man, naked as herself, and staring at her with dazed and astounded eyes.

It was Major Ledyard Houghton.

iii

Her first impulse was to turn and run. But that was one too ridiculous to follow. Absurdly, she remembered a story from some Victorian romance of the heroine, nude, discovered by a man, and the modest female covering her face with her hands to hide her *identity*. . . . She giggled and sank down on the grass.

'Thank goodness there's someone else in this mess. But however have we got into it?'

'Damned if I know. I woke and saw you swimming down there . . . if I am awake.'

'Don't worry about that. I've thought it all out for myself, and you can take the results on trust. But I do wish you'd sit down.'

'Why?'

Gay clasped her knees with her hands. 'So that we can talk. And you're rather — undraped.'

He had an exceedingly white skin. It turned a rich crimson, face, neck. . . . Gay turned away her eyes, politely, from survey of its further possibilities. He slumped down in the grass.

'Oh, damn it!'

He leapt up again. He had sat on a gorse-bush. Gay put up her hands to her eyes and giggled helplessly.

Giggling, she heard him say, hardly, 'If you've got hysterics, you can get out of them. I'm off to see what's happened.'

He was. He had jumped to his feet again. He had broad shoulders and shapely hips, except for one with a great scar, like that of a branding-iron, across it. Gay stared at the scar, herself standing up.

'Where can you go? . . . And where did that happen to you?'

He stared over his shoulder, angry and ludicrous. 'Eh? What? What happen?' He coloured again, richly. 'War-time wound.'

'I see. And where are you going?'

'To find . . . ' he stared around, 'some house.'

'Does it look as though there are any?'

It did not. The fact seemed to sink into their unevenly beating hearts. It was a land wild and forgotten. No human feet had trodden it, or voices called here, or the busy world of men reached out a hand here for long ages. The sunlight ran its colours up and down the near hills, gay with gorse. Far off a peewit wailed its immemorial plaint. There was no mark of cultivation or sign of human kind. Gay said, very quietly:

'Something has happened to us. I don't know what. But we're here, lost, as though we'd been newly born. If we're going to search out anything, perhaps we'd best do it together.' She shaded her eyes with her hand, looking towards the tumuli. Without much hope: 'There might be something to help us in those mounds.'

They set out, almost side by side, across the spring of the grass. In Gay's mind was a bubbling tumult of thought and speculation, backgrounded by a horrible fear which she closed away. That wouldn't help, she'd to keep sane; and keep up with the headache man; and be thankful she'd a decent figure under these shy-making circumstances.

She glanced down at it, nicely browned, and felt absurdly cheered. Houghton swung beside her in silence, his neat, thinned Greek profile rigidly towards her, his eyes fixed ahead. She suddenly realised that he was elaborately and painstakingly *not* looking at her. Also, that he was wishing, with an angry embarrassment, that she would not look at him.

They came in silence to the foot of the great mounds. There were three of them, matted in long, coarse grass. Gay went through the space between the nearer two and saw beyond merely such rolling hill-country, rolling deserted to the horizon's edge, as lay to the west. She heard Houghton breathing, coming round the corner.

'They're just hills.'

Gay shook her head. 'Mounds, I think. I've dug ancient ones in Mexico, and they've much these shapes, ruined buildings with a thousand years or so of the blowing of sand and earth on the top of them . . .' She stopped, appalled. 'Oh, God!'

He barked, 'Eh?' — it must have been his tribal war-cry — staring about him. But Gay was merely looking blankly at the mounds. She said:

'I don't know much of the Pewsey country, but there were no mounds near the village last night. None marked on any archaeological map. If these have taken years to accumulate, then . . .'

For the first time their eyes met, and she saw herself globed in the light grey eyes of Houghton — shallow, puzzled eyes, faintly red-rimmed. She saw her face, strained and white, in that reflection, above her brown throat. . . . Houghton looked away.

'Then this can't be the Pewsey district.'

'But it is. That hill over there — I saw it as I went to sleep last night — if it was last night.' She felt suddenly breathless and sat down. 'Listen, what did you do when *you* went to bed last night?'

'What? Tried the formula of this Dunne rubbish you talked about.'

'Did you have any success?' Gay's voice sounded far away to herself.

23

'Stuff like nightmare after a bit. Half-dozing, I suppose. The lightning cracked into the stuff and made my headache twice as bad. Then I slipped into the stuff again – damned rubbish. Woke up and saw you.'

'This rubbishy dream stuff – did you have a sensation of going at a tremendous rate – slipping over the brink of a precipice?'

He scowled in thought. 'No. Something – like going up a spiral staircase, and lights winking in and out from the windows. Anyhow, what does it matter? What's it to do with this – blasted insanity?'

'I'm not sure – yet.' Gay Hunter still felt breathless. That, and queer, as though she was about to be sick. 'But I've a guess – oh, hell 'n' blast, it can't be, it can't be!'

'All this is rot to me. Look here, if we're going together, we might as well start. I'm going on – to get clothes somewhere, and back to London, whatever has happened here in Wiltshire.'

Gay stood up, slowly, a queer look on her face. 'All right? East?'

'That's the direction of London, isn't it?'

'Yes, that's the direction of London. Or was.'

'Eh?'

She gripped his naked arm. 'What's *that*?'

That was a movement in the long grass at a distance of ten yards or so from the mounds – a movement that ended in a tall, blonde woman, unclad as themselves, with a scared, astounded face, rising into full view and staring at them with horrified eyes. Gay blinked her own eyes at the sight. Had the whole damn landscape been showered with undraped females in the night? O Lord, she was going mad. . . .

'Ledyard!'

Houghton stood halted, staring, a dismayed, agonised, smoking-room-story blush in effigy.

'Jane!'

Gay slumped down in the grass, too wearied with surprises even to giggle. 'Do introduce us.'

'Eh? What? Oh *Lord*, Jane! . . . This is Lady Jane Easterling, Miss Hunter.'

So that was how.

Lady Jane Easterling, her hysterical story brought to an hysterical end, was now sobbing into her hands, having nothing else to sob into. Houghton was patting her shoulder, tentatively. Gay, for lack of the consolation of either pat or sob, pulled a long grass and bit at it, and stared at her own shaking fingers.

So that was how ...

It has been a confused enough story (she was the kind of spoilt woman who confused stories and most other things, Gay thought, with a slight cattishness), but the main outlines not too blurred. Lady Jane the lady patroness of the local Fascists.... Lady Jane with a house near Pewsey.... Houghton a guest at her house. . . . A tiff. . . . Houghton off on a propaganda walking tour . . . Houghton and his headaches brought back to Pewsey in the Morgan.... Houghton making the compact for a neo-Dunne test with an impertinent American girl, and then ringing up Lady Jane from the hotel and the two of them indulging in an orgy of reconciliation over the telephone – an orgy in which Houghton had told this bored, idle woman of the method by which he was to seek sleep. And Lady Jane, being bored, had gone to bed and amused herself in like manner....

(Oh hell 'n' blast, Daddy, *what* a mess! And to think I once laughed at you when you talked of the risks of neo-Dunne!)

The sobs were dying away. Certainly a lovely sobber – a little younger than Houghton, perhaps, pre-Raphaelitish even to the short, haughty lip; white and gold.... Houghton was proving consoling.

'This is just some idiot accident, Jane – some local upset in conditions. We'll push east and soon get help, Reading or London or nearer.'

'Oh Ledyard, you're sure? I'd go mad in this desert.... And all through the filthy trick this girl started you on!'

'Rubbish, nothing to do with that stuff. Eh, Miss Hunter?'

Gay shook her head, standing up. 'Let's set out. Nothing? Sorry. I'm afraid it's got everything.'

3. Even the Stars

THEY HALTED that night on the fringes of a great forest east of Pewsey. Perhaps this was where Kingsclere once had been. Treading through the long grass, they neared the black cluster of trees, gigantic in the departing light of the sun. When near, they saw they were of an unknown species, tall, smooth-trunked, like giant wands, and bearing far on their crests clusters of plumage like palms. That plumage was waving and whispering in the summer wind, and they saw far down, treey aisles to distances where the light failed completely. In those dim depths the ground was carpeted with a pine-needle-like detritus. Gay halted, staring down a corridor.

'Better not go in.'

Gasping, Lady Jane sank down at the foot of the nearest tree. Houghton glanced over his shoulder, breathing deeply. 'No.'

Gay also looked back. But the giant bear which had roused them from their berry-picking a mile or so away was nowhere in sight. Gay raised her head, crushing the wild strawberries into a hungry mouth, her lips red with the stain of them, to glance at Houghton, and Lady Jane, and had caught sight of the horrified apprehension in their eyes. Then she had looked over her shoulder and seen the great bear — the size and shape of a polar bear, but brown — snuffling on its hind-legs and waving its head and shoulders to and fro, undecidedly. Gay had never been aware she could run so quickly. She had almost overtaken Lady Jane. Then she had halted and looked back. Houghton was cursing the bear shakily, and standing in its path, covering their retreat. Oh, the damn fool. . . .

She had run back and seized his arm. 'Come on, you idiot!'

26

He had said, 'Run, damn you!' and to the bear, 'Get off!'
The bear had yawned. They had turned and run together.
Beyond the patch all three had looked back and seen the
beast following them, at a canter, snuffling in their tracks, the
hair about its neck erected in a ruff. Gay had glanced down at
her heels and understood. She was leaving a trail of
blood-specks from a thorn-scratch. She had stooped and
wiped her heel. When next she had looked back, the bear was
halted, on its hind-legs, pawing the air again. It had lost the
trail.

Now they must find somewhere to put up for the night.

Houghton was evidently thinking the same. 'But where?
There's been no sign of a house all day.'

No house; no people; no sign of a railway track; no sign of
grazing kine or the smoke from a harvester's pipe; no sign of
roads or rails or all the busy life of the world. At noon, by a
spring that burst from the earth, they had halted to eat wild
plums — plums growing from the side of just such another
tumulus as reared its head by the place where they awoke.
Pulling at a cluster of plums, Gay had pulled away with it a
clot of earth, and something that had for a moment a shape,
and then fell into a handful of dust. She had caught up a little
of that dust and examined it. Lady Jane regarded her with a
cold distaste. But Houghton came to look — with less strain in
her presence than in the early morning. Already, she had
thought, raising her head and glancing at him, they were
accepting each other, naked and ashamed, with indifference.
(Thanks, perhaps, to Lady Jane's chilling chaperonage.) He
had asked: 'What is it?'

She could tell him that. 'Iron-dust.'

'Iron-dust?'

'Yes. It goes readily.' She had peered into the tumulus wall,
and then shivered in spite of herself. 'Part of a railway
embankment, perhaps.'

'What? That's rot, of course.'

She had nodded. 'Yes, Rotten iron.'

'Miss Hunter is a wag, Ledyard.'

Just after they finished their meal he had jumped to his feet
and started to rave, beating his head with his hands,
and going lurching like a blind man among the mounds.

27

Lady Jane had run after him, startled. Gay had paused in her berry-munching and regarded him, bored.

'Stop it, Mr. Houghton!'

He had stopped, wheeling on her with murder in his eyes. She had felt a quake of fear, what of this size and that look.

'Stop it! Who began it? You and this damned experiment that has pitched us into this nightmare. Stop it? By God, I've a good mind to wring your neck.'

She had glanced from his maddened face to Lady Jane's expectant one (how the woman *did* detest her!), then round the silent, deserted countryside, eerie in its quietness under the noonday fall of sun:

'You two would find yourselves rather lonely if you did.'

That had quietened him. He took shape as a bully almost automatically —a courageous bully, however, Gay thought as they stood now and peered in the depths of the sunset forest. Most bullies, in fact, were courageous — a horrid moral mistake!

The light grew dimmer while they hesitated. Then Gay said 'Listen!' very softly.

It came from far away in the depths of the forest — remote and strange and lovely, drowsily and clearly, the croon of a ring-dove's note. Houghton glared impatiently towards the sound.

'Only a dove.'

'I know. But it might have been a condor.... What are you going to do now?'

'Damned if I know.' His hand wandered up to his head, and then hesitated. 'Funny. I haven't had a spot of headaches since....'

'Since the nightmare began. Perhaps one doesn't have headaches in nightmares. I'm going to camp just here, anyway.'

Lady Jane lay exhausted where she had fallen, at the foot of the nearest tree. She was sobbing again. Houghton went towards her, diffidently, and bent down with a hand on her white shoulder:

'Jane....'

Gay turned to her bedmaking. She was scratched and tired and had no one to take her shoulder and say 'Gay' in a soothing Oxford ha-ha. But, absurdly, she felt almost happy. A sudden lift of the wind sent all the plumage, the silky plumage of the strange forest trees, quivering with a strange moaning sound. She looked up at those ferny crowns and down through the dark corridors again.

What lay within or beyond?

And suddenly she knew it was nothing terrifying, even though it might be a pack of wild beasts of unknown shape and ravenousness. They could do no more at the utmost than kill her and eat her! And, she thought philosophically, while she pulled the long grass and twisted it into shape for a pillow, hadn't that happened often enough to others since the first men came wandering into Europe twenty thousand years before? Naked and lost in an impossible countryside in an impossible England — it was now you realised how little and how much your life was worth. All the fears and dreads you ever had had been for the things you now lacked: clothes and books and cigarettes and jewels and marcel waves and sweets — not for yourself at all!

She stood upright, panting a little, taking her breath while she thought that: she had no more fear of the world, naked and lost, than a naked baby new-born!

Lady Jane was being consoled. They were having a perfect orgy, Gay thought with a little twinge of lostness, in spite of her genial assurance to herself. Nice to have someone cuddle you, discreetly, and tell you it was all right, and they'd soon reach some place with clothes and food.

When they wouldn't.

Beyond the murmur of the voices of Lady Jane and Houghton she heard the trill of a stream and felt suddenly thirsty. She called, 'I'm going for a drink,' and went down the edge of the trees by a little hill. Here, in the sunset, she came on the stream, osier-fringed, with a clear, sandy bed. Against that bed she saw trout gliding. Presently the reeds at the other side broke and a water-hen sailed out and across the slow flow. Gay looked after it, and then, bending to drink as an animal drinks, caught sight of herself.

She considered that self for a little while, and saw her lips quiver. Damn young to be launched out in the wastes of

29

time and space, with a vexing intelligence; and without any cuddles.

The light was dying as she took her way back by the tree-boles. The sun burned like a far fire down through the remote tree-corridors. Lady Jane sat shivering and cuddling herself under her tree while Houghton, with some deftness, arranged a shelter of broken plumage-branches he had collected from the forest floor. He said, 'Where have you been?'

Gay's voice was equally low: 'Having a drink. There's a stream down there.'

'Oh! And I — I feel so dreadfully thirsty.' Lady Jane's throaty contralto, starting on its normal note, trailed into a murmurous wail. Houghton glanced from her to Gay. The latter hesitated a moment. Then:

'The water's quite close. There's no danger.'

She could feel their gaze on her back as she went to her bed. Lady Jane drawled, with a sudden return to normality:

'What a funny and charming accent! Did you say it was New York you came from, Miss Hunter — the Bowery?'

Gay lay down and yawned, and pulled the blanketing swathes of grass over herself. 'Pity you weren't properly smacked in your young days, Lady Jane. Good night.'

There was a silence. Then Houghton said: 'Er — good night.' Presently Gay heard a rustling of grass, and looking rightwards saw them disappear down towards the stream.

Had a nice figure, the girl. Pity she was the type she was. Funniest kind of parasite ever evolved by the species in these modern days. . . .

These modern days!

What days were they? She cuddled the grass closer up to her chin and watched the sky. Slowly the painted colours of the sunset faded off. A deep grey followed and then more slowly all the horizon rims grew black. Darkness came flowing out from the forest, wave on wave. Far off among the trees an owl hooted, oddly homely the sound. The black of the sky was changing to a deep blue. Gay heard the sound of the footsteps of Houghton and Lady Jane returning through the grass. She lay quiet.

Where were they? And what time were they in? What would they find to-morrow?

She knew quite well what had happened — it was something like this her father must have feared, when he spoke of risks and precautions. They had dreamt themselves forward into the times to be, through the dusty curtain that overhung the future of the twentieth century. Something propitious in the air and conditions of last night — if one could think of it as last night! What night had it been, the last one to come down over this wild land where condors and bears wandered, and palm-trees were roofed like pines? And how far from that evening in Pewsey when the three of them had last seen sunset?

Fifty years? A hundred? More than that. The country had changed beyond recognition, the two English people said. For roads and railways to disappear argued the passage of a great stretch of years. It was easy to say that to oneself, cuddling down here in the warmth of the grass — easy, unless one realised that this self one loved and liked and laughed at was — lost in the deeps of time, unbefriended, in a world where the men who survived might be an alien and a terrifying species. Beyond that forest.

Beyond that forest.

She turned over on her shoulder to look at it. It was quiet and voiceless. What lay beyond — what strange world of men in this lost century? She thought of books of speculation she had read on the future — books of the early Wells, of Flammarion, of their hosts of imitators: books that pictured the sciences mounting and growing, piling great crystalline pyramids of knowledge and technique into alien skies, with men their servitors, changing and altering with them, physically and psychically, mislaying legs and intestinal tubes, sprouting many arms, becoming bisexual, becoming as strange and repulsive gods dominating a strange and repulsive earth. She thought of the fantastic beings of a play, *Back to Methuselah,* by one of the quack prophets of that remote time — the remote time in which she herself was born! — who were bred to long lives of thousands of years and spent them in meditation on the Oneness of Life! What a eunuch's dream! Or the younger Huxley, with a machine-made world and machine-made humans, undergoing a fantastic existence conditioned of the bleak lunacy of their author's anthropological beliefs.... Worlds without end that had been foisted upon the future. And which, if any, had that world accepted?

She thought of another who had stirred the historical dovecotes of her time — Spengler, with his theories of cyclic catastrophe, or the rise and fall of cultures, inevitable and unceasing. His slick, quack arguments, built of poor reasoning and worse research had left her unmoved, but how they had moved her contemporary world! What a brainless and barren world that had been, headlessly searching for a way of life! How had they solved it, what had happened to them? To Roosevelt and Hitler and Mussolini and Stalin and Theodore Dreiser and Frau Krupp and Chiang Kai-shek and Pavlov and Einstein and the prostitutes in Broadway and the publishers in Fourth Avenue and the war-lunatics in the asylums and the little folk on the Middle West farms and the landlord of the 'Peacock'—and all they suffered and believed and imagined undying, tremendous, divine? How had the centuries dealt with them? ...

Beyond the forest, to-morrow.

The stars were coming. The Milky Way was banded tremendous across the sky. She moved her head and looked where the North Star pointed as of yore — but was it quite as of yore? She felt her heart beat high in her chest as she looked, crouched upon her elbow.

For Charles's Wain had altered his ancient shape — he bulged more steeply up the sky, as though smitten a great upwards blow. Her eyes wandered from constellation to constellation. In Hercules she saw a great star shine that had not been there last night....

Last night! Oh, God, how many nights ago? Before the stars altered their shaping and grouping hundreds and hundreds of years must have passed. Hundreds? Thousands, rather. So many that they might never learn — so many that the human race might have grown incomprehensible, alien, strange beings who would slaughter them as unclean animals, as German peasants of the twentieth century would have slaughtered a Heidelberg man had he arisen,

32

great-browed and chinless, unmummified from some primal pit. Oh God!

And, as she crouched there in terror, slowly the moon topped the strange forest. Its light came down the corridor of trees and she saw it high and golden, and laid her head in her hands and wept.

It was nearer, larger, *a different moon.*

ii

In the middle of the night she awakened to the sound of a scream. It was the voice of Lady Jane, uplifted in that oddly asinine, cultured haw:

'Help, Help! Ledyard!'

Gay leapt to her feet and found the night a cold shower of a night — it was as though she had leapt out under a cold shower. The moon was sinking and, in its light, grass-scattering a little distance away, she saw Houghton rise up as well. Lady Jane, hand at mouth, was screaming wordlessly.

They saw the reason. A great black panther which had come out of the forest and awakened Lady Jane by licking her nose. The scrape of its tongue had brought her out of sleep to the glare of two tremendous, yellow eyes above her. The beast had sprung away, and stood now coal-black and tail-switching in the moonlight.

Houghton and Gay recovered simultaneously. They shouted and made at the panther. It could have made mincemeat of both of them. Instead, with a surprised *fuf!* it turned and slunk away through the tree-boles. They halted, panting, Houghton trembling and flaring.

'Blasted stink-cat!'

Lady Jane was in hysterics. Gay walked over and prodded her ribs and legs in search of wounds, and put up a hand to her face. Instantly her hand was bitten. She pulled it away, and administered a slap which instantly finished the hysterics. Instantly she found Houghton beside her.

'You callous little bitch! What are you hitting her for?'

33

Gay yawned sleepily. 'To keep her quiet.'

'If you yourself . . . '

'If I'd been rescued from an amour with a pussycat I'd keep quiet about it.' She felt both sleepy and tired. Also, suddenly, she wanted to cry. 'I'm going back to bed.'

'You can go to the devil.'

Such a funny little squabble under the sinking of that alien moon, the strange world, tenebrous, awaiting a momentous dawn!

iii

In the early morning she found the plovers' eggs.

She had been roused by the cheep of sparrows, pecking within a foot of her head, and, rousing, had remembered instantly where she was. Sparrows! But of course they would hardly change — sparrows and swallows were almost eternal, unless the great steaming jungles came back to the earth. She lay in the quietude of the dawn and looked at the little birds. The dew was sparkling. Beyond the chirping of the sparrows, far off, a peewit wailed.

She got to her feet and looked towards the place where Lady Jane slept, and then towards the spot where Houghton had lain down the previous night. The latter spot was a ruffled straw desertion. Up already? Then she saw that Houghton and Lady Jane, inadequately shielded by their covering of grass, were sleeping in each other's arms.

Sensible people. For the first time in her acquaintance with them in the last twenty-four hours, she felt friendly towards them. Looked nice, cuddled there.

She took her way down towards the stream where she had drunk last night. A little mist ebbed away from its banks. The water was icy cold as she plunged into it and squatted and paddled, for it was not deep enough for her to swim. As she squatted and splashed and rubbed the night-time tiredness and hayseed dust from her skin she felt her back tickled by the flirting tails of the little trout. Friendly little beasts.

She got out on the bank and wiped herself with her hands,

34

inadequately, glanced back and upwards towards where the other two slept, and then turned and ran down by the forest edge, in the sunlight, running to dry herself.

Presently the fun of that carried her feet to racing speed. She fled her own shadow into the west, over the tussocky grass, running light and free —goodness, never so free before in her life! Running, she was aware of all her body pringling to life, and sank down at last by a solitary bush in the plain, panting, her skin quivering, dry and comfortable and a very good skin. She remembered the stick and cling of even the scantiest bathing-dresses, and how she had always loathed them. Freed from that, anyhow.

Then she heard something panting at her elbow, and turned her head.

Running, she had half-imagined she heard the scamper of feet behind her. Now it was plain it had been no imagining. The beast sat a yard away, regarding her with laughing eyes, with tongue lolling out and quivering, serrated jaw-skin. Gay forgot the entire strangeness of the place and time.

'Why, you dear!'

It was only as she put her arms round his neck and cuddled him that she realised what she had done. The brute was no dog: it was a wolf.

Her arms stiffened. Thereat the wolf licked her intimately, so that it tickled. Gay laughed. Unbelievable, but a fact. He was tame!

They sat and regarded each other with great friendliness. The bigness of a wolf, dark-grey, with a wavy yellow stripe along the belly, the wolf or dog had a bright, inquisitive right ear and a drooping left one apparently badly mangled in some encounter. His gaze on Gay was not the bland, eager gaze of a dog, however, but a gay, friendly, independent one. What freak beast was it?

'You may have had a master, but he's left no mark. Or are you just amused and tickled to see a member of the Americanist Conference of the twentieth century running about unclad in your own?...Well, what are you going to do?'

The great beast had got to its feet. It looked as big as a St. Bernard. It glanced at Gay, snuffled the air, and prepared to depart.

'Don't, for goodness' sake. Couldn't you dig out some breakfast for me, seeing I've come such a long way?'

Absurdly he seemed to understand. He trotted away, back towards the stream, turning his head every now and then to see if she followed. Close by the stream the air whirred and fluttered with plovers' wings. The beast nosed about in the grass, sat down, and began a rapid and enjoyable scrunching. Gay peered over his shoulder. It was a plovers' nest.

They finished off the raw eggs between them. Wiping her small mouth, Gay remembered Houghton and Lady Jane and searched for another nest. Presently she found one with three eggs and set out up the stream. The beast trotted in front of her, halted, stiffed. Gay topped the rise to see Lady Jane and Houghton just about to enter the avenue of pine-palms together. At the scuffle of the beast's approach they halted. Gay did the same.

'Going to leave me?'

'We thought you had left us.'

This was Houghton. But he had flushed dully. Lady Jane shrank behind him at the sight of the wolf, till Gay called out he was tame. He went up and sniffed delicately at the heels of the two, then sneezed profoundly, and turned a questioning head to Gay.

'All right, friends — more or less.... I've brought you people some eggs.'

Lady Jane stared at them in distaste. She looked very lovely, Gay thought. White and gold. 'But however are we going to eat them?'

'Suck them, the same as your grandmother.'

Even naked, Lady Jane could smile an aloof amusement for such gawkish flippancy. And now, lowering her eyes a little from that fine face and torso, Gay saw that she was no longer naked. In the morning or during the evening she had woven a grass and rush skirt, now draped round her waist and reaching to within two inches of her knees. Lady Jane nodded.

'Don't you think you'd better do the same?'

Gay glanced at Houghton. The shameful portion of his anatomy also was concealed. Abruptly the situation had changed. They were two people clad, with responsibilities, and already poise, even while they stood and sucked raw

36

eggs. Gay realised suddenly the nakedness of her smooth skin under that appraising glance of Lady Jane, and for a minute felt daunted. Then she glanced again at the grass skirts and began to giggle, very helplessly. The wolf-beast snuffled and came and licked her shoulder as she sat down. Gay wiped her eyes.

'Sorry, but you both look as funny as ... And why bother with the things? Especially in this weather?'

'We'll soon be nearing London, and there's bound to be people about,' Houghton said. Lady Jane was looking at Gay with coolly upraised brows.

'Elementary decency — especially when you have such an oddly brown figure.'

Gay nodded to her with a little smile. 'We *do* detest each other, don't we? Especially as you know that I have rather a nice figure — intriguing, not just obviously lovely, like yours. But, frankly, I think you look indecent in these things. I'm a human being — but you two look like savages. Even in London you'll look older than I. Especially ...'

'Yes?' Lady Jane Easterling wiped her mouth, as delicately as she might, with a bunch of grass.

'Did either of you look at the stars last night?'

'The stars?' What on earth for, my good girl?'

Gay shrugged. 'Oh, well. Look at them to-night and they'll tell you things. Rather appalling things, I imagine. Here, Wolf!'

The beast had wandered off, tree-investigatory, in the old canine convention. Some things survived even the moving of the stars.... Now it stopped and regarded Gay with a bright, humorous eye. She resolved to trust to its leading, rather than the opinions of the lady secretary and organiser of the Fascist Defence Corps.

She and the wolf entered the forest together.

Lady Jane Easterling and Houghton looked at each other, then followed.

iv

For a space of two miles or more they trod down those

forest corridors on a carpet of pine-humus. Here the light, even the early light of morning, came but dimly, and the air was choked with the acrid smell of the trees —the smell of pine and palm commingled (and poor old Kipling not here to ecstasize!). The wolf scampered ahead and then came back now and then to pad by Gay's side. Once she ruffled his head and at that he snapped at her, with gleaming teeth, only just missing her finger. Not so tame. She went on more soberly by his side.

Then, and very suddenly, the forest opened into a great wide space, circular, tree-guarded, without grass or bush or growing thing. It was an uneven, undulating surface, a surface of blown cones and rotted tree-plumage, but somehow Gay had the notion of its perfect flatness underneath that earthy deposit. One of the pine-plumes had fallen near at hand. She picked it up and on a sudden impulse began to dig through the humus.

The wolf halted and sat down, watching. Houghton and Lady Jane came up. Lady Jane raised amused eyebrows:

'Whatever are you at, now?'

She spoke as to a somewhat disgusting child. Gay continued to dig. At a depth of about a foot and a half the plume branch scraped sharply, as on metal. Gay enlarged the hold, flinging out the dirt with her hands. Nor had she been mistaken. Under her eyes shone a dull gleam. She scratched it — the green encrustation. It was copper, or some alloy of copper.

She told that to Houghton and he bent and looked. It was an eerie place. A great circular flooring of copper lay here in the midst of this lost forest — for what, by whom placed there? Lady Jane Easterling moved impatiently.

'Oh, do let's go on. What does it matter though there's copper here? It's no use to us.'

'No.' Houghton assented. But he was evidently worried by that great stretch of treeless, bushless track, as they left it behind. He cleared his throat, addressing Gay with difficulty.

'If you would mind telling us, Miss Hunter — what was it that was peculiar in the sky last night?'

Gay glanced at him with a smile, a smile of sympathy. Poor man. Lady Jane's man. Poor in both respects! But

38

relations were strained enough without saying so. Instead:

'Just that the moon's larger—that means nearer than it used to be — and that one or two of the constellations have altered shape. You know what that means?'

'I think so.' He obviously knew nothing about it. Lady Jane was listening with her usual polite amusement to this boring and loquacious child. Gay, swinging forward in that jaunty schoolboy stride of hers, sought carefully for the right phrases:

'It's just that we aren't in the twentieth century at all. In the neo-Dunne test we all three went beyond it by some accident. We're far in the future. Stars don't alter their appearance and grouping from the surface of the earth until the passing of long ages. And the moon was nearing the earth very slowly in the twentieth century — a foot or so every hundred years, I think. It means that we're in a time at least as remote from the twentieth century as it was from the days of the people who built the Egyptian pyramids — more probably far remoter.'

Even Lady Jane understood this. She said, incredulously: 'And what is the rest of the fairy-tale, Miss Hunter?'

Gay shrugged: 'Oh, a country without roads or railroads or houses. With polar bears turned brown. With black panthers licking people's noses at nights —with this wolf, here.'

Houghton's brick-red face had paled. 'You really believe, Miss Hunter, that we've travelled forward through time?'

Gay felt an odd compassion for him. 'I know we have.'

'Then — my God, Jane, there mayn't be any purpose going east. There mayn't be even London there.'

'Nonsense, of course there is.' But she had begun to drag, sore-footed. 'If only I had shoes.'

Gay was humming. Houghton said, irritably: 'For God's sake, would you mind shutting that off or else singing it aloud? It's getting on my nerves.'

Gay said 'Sure,' and raised her voice. The wolf came growling to her side. The forest stirred from its sleep — how long since it had heard a human voice raised in singing?

> 'Gay go up and Gay go down:
> That is the way to London Town!'

39

4. The Mounds of Windsor

i

BUT THEY did not make London that day. They were not to make London for many days. For beyond the forest — they reached its boundaries when the summer sun stood high at noon — something bright red and shifting, vermilion, a smoulder down in the east, caught Gay's eyes. She stopped and looked at it, a hand to her eyes, her hair blown about her head, a brown, sturdy figure in the flow and wisp of great cloud masses rolling down from the north. Summer rain coming. But what was that thing in the east?

Houghton and Lady Jane also wondered that. They stood a long while, the three of them, staring and speculating, Gay perforce included in the group in the puzzlement of the moment. She dropped her hand with a sigh.

'Miles away. We'll just have to walk on till we see. Meanwhile, I'm hungry.'

Lady Jane sank down. '*Do* see if there's any fruit, Ledyard.'

The wolf had disappeared. Presently, as Gay and Houghton spread out through the grass, rather hopelessly, for they seemed to have come to a wide, bushless stretch of llano, he came shivering the grasses and laid something at Gay's feet. It was a large buck hare — a perfect small deer of a thing. Gay's mouth watered.

'You're a dear. But we've no fire. Couldn't you dig out a basket of strawberries instead?'

The wolf lay down and rubbed his nose on his paws, and snuffled, still regarding Gay with his unwinking gaze. She patted his head, thoughtlessly, forgetting how he had snapped at her. But this time he endured it, philosophically. She called to Houghton and held up the hare to his gaze. His protest was a repetition of hers to the wolf.

'But we've no fire.'

'I know. But that thing over there' — she pointed to the wandering vermilion flicker that rode the horizon where once Sandhurst or Wokingham had been —'looks like fire of some kind. Suppose we tramp on and see? There are no berries here.'

That was self-evident. Gay carrying the hare, they returned to where Lady Jane Easterling was squatted upon the grass. She had plucked more grasses and was busily plaiting them. Houghton explained Gay's proposal.

'But I can't possibly. I'm too tired to walk a step.'

'Afraid you'll just have to.' Houghton was suddenly, to her, for the first time brusque. 'There's nothing else for it.'

Lady Jane displayed a sudden common sense. Gay abruptly realised that the woman was, in her own way, adapting herself to conditions just as rapidly and completely as that naked brown figure which clothed itself in the name of Gay Hunter. 'Oh, right.' She regarded her plaiting with some anxiety. 'Go right now, what?'

'We'd better,' Houghton growled. 'I'm hungry.'

They set out through the grass. Looking back at the end of half an hour or so Gay saw the strange forest sinking down on the skyline in the west. The vermilion flicker grew brighter in the east. Now they saw that it held all the forward skyline, not alone, but ran in a thin vignetting of colour southwards as well. They were walking into an angle of the thing. Still it was impossible to name it.

Gay's feet and thighs began to ache. Presently she breathed with some difficulty and saw that it was the same with the two stray Fascists. Abruptly the wolf halted, so that Gay nearly stumbled over him. He was smelling the east. Now he refused to go further.

Gay coaxed him for a little while, while Houghton and Lady Jane went on. Then she gave him a last pat, and went after the other two, once turning to wave to the friendly, unaccountable beast. Presently she heard a long-drawn wolf-howl diminuendoing into the north.

41

So, in the early afternoon, they came through the last of the grass and crossed a waste stretch of land, long burned black of all vegetation, the very mould and the earth consumed, leaving only the primal rocks, and came to the verge of the great depression in which played unceasingly the vermilion flame. The air even at that great distance — for it was many miles away in the heart of the great saucer-shaped depression that the flame played —was alive with cracklings and spittings, and a waft of wind blew on them once a whiff of mephitic gas which caused Houghton to cough and cough until he was coughing blood, and vexed even the normal lungs of Gay and Lady Jane. Then, treading as near to the edge as they might, they looked across the great gulf that yawned where once the rich wooded lands of Wokingham waved green.

Suddenly, in some far time, and for an area of many miles, the earth had vomited upon the heavens, leaving a great cavity where mist and fire now played in remote and scattered pools. Only the distance of the forest fringe had led them to believe the line of fire was continuous. Now they saw it as the joint effect of a score of craterlets in the boiling tumult of the interior. Continually the air shook.

For a long time Houghton and Lady Jane found it too appalling for words. Gay had half expected that something like this had fathered the winking vermilion light they had seen on the horizon. But, even expecting it, the reality was dreadful enough. She had dropped the hare and put up both hands this time to peer across that hellish gulf in the green lands of England. But the crater mists cut off all view of the other side. It might stretch for a dozen miles.

Lady Jane said suddenly, startling them all: 'It's horrible. But I'm still sickeningly hungry.'

Houghton tried to speak, coughed again, tried again, and succeeded.

'And that fire's too far off for any hope of cooking. Impossible to go down there. Miss Hunter — don't be a fool!'

Gay had started off, hare in hand, towards the crumbling black edge of the great saucer. Something there, a rise and flow of the earth, had attracted her attention. She stepped cautiously, barely cautiously enough. Suddenly the earth gave way under an advancing foot. She leapt back just in time, for with a slither and gurgle the surface flowed away. Steaming, a spout of mud arose from the ground and poured over the black brink. Gay put down her hand and then withdrew it. No need to touch it. It was boiling.

She turned and called to the other two.

'Very handy. We can cook the hare here.'

iii

All that day, as the afternoon wore to evening, they coasted northwards, seeking to escape round the rim of the great depression. Distant to the right, unbegun, unending, the muffled explosions went on in the craterlets. Riding those gusty sounds came once a shower of rain —boiling rain that scorched their bodies so that they cried out and ran, and thereafter drew further from the lip of the saucer, into country where the waste grassland presently changed character into straggling clumps of beech trees. Here great mounds rose from the earth in the evening light and here, twisting amidst these mounds, they came to the bank of a stream. Something in the shape of the place as the light drew in caught Houghton's attention. He stopped and stared and then turned to Lady Jane.

'By God,' he said, 'It's Windsor.'

Gay had never been there before. But now she sought back in history-book lessons. 'Didn't your kings once live here?'

Houghton's hand went up to his face, to wipe his forehead. 'I had a brother on guard-duty here last . . . ' he swore shakily, 'I was going to say last week.'

Lady Jane shivered. 'Oh, it's a nightmare, it's impossible! Where are we going to shelter?'

Remote to the right the great fires were now pringling the darkness. The sky had become overcast. Gay, searching amidst the mounds, found a place where a thin stream ran down to meet that attenuated Thames. She called to the others and they came and stood beside her.

It was a sloping hole in the earth. Houghton got down on his hands and knees and crawled within. Presently his heels re-emerged.

'It's a room — once the room of a house. I think we'll be all right in here.'

They crept in. As they did so the last of the daylight went. Crawling in, Gay heard a low swish of disturbed grass and a patter of multitudinous feet. It was the coming of the rain. Her hand encountered a leg. Lady Jane said, 'Would you mind not clawing me?'

'Sorry.'

They crouched in darkness for a little while, listening to each other's breathing and the blind fall of the rain outside. Then suddenly a great flare of sheet lightning ran amidst the Windsor mounds and fizzled and crackled at the door of their cave. Shielding her eyes from the bite of the light, Gay saw their shelter flood-lighted a moment.

A great enduring pillar of stone lay drunkenly athwart the roof. That it was which held up the masses of débris — had held them up through many ages. The walls were the merest slabs of bare rock, worn away by time even in this place untouched of wind and rain. And beside the place where she crouched lay a half-eaten human cadaver.

At first she thought that a trick of her eyesight, then lightning flared again and, for a long moment, with a cool dispassion, she sat and stared at the thing beside her. It had been a man — it was the mummified body of a man, the face shrivelled, the eyes starting horribly from the head, the neck pinched black, a ghastly simulacrum of humanity. Beasts had devoured a great stretch of the stomach, but she saw even the torn intestines twisted black, as though an acid had been poured in them. She stared in frozen horror.

Houghton and Lady Jane had also seen it. Lady Jane screamed, piercingly, and made for the entrance. Houghton swore shakily, cried to her to stop, dived after her. The next flame of light that came at the entrance to the shelter showed no trace of them. Gay crouched in a shivering indecision.

If the beast that had been tearing this body came back?

Crouching, she made for the entrance. In that moment the lightning again flared, forked lightning this time, and suddenly the shelter quivered and rocked and was blinded of light. Rock débris and earth fell on her hands and face. A slithering rumble fell away into the night.

A landfall had closed up the cave entrance.

Gay heard the cadaver snuffle beside her, and the hair rose at the back of her neck. She set her teeth against that imagining, heard again the snuffle, and fainted.

iv

It seemed to her many hours afterwards when she awoke. It was pitch-dark still, and the air had grown close and dank, many times breathed and re-breathed. She put out a hand against the encompassing wall of darkness, and then drew it back with a cry, for it had touched the face of the mummy.

She sat and shivered, trying to think. Surely Houghton would come back and clear away the earthfall? Would he? Would he know what place to try? Would he care to? Was he himself still alive?

Now the air grew still more stifling. Presently she drowsed away again into unconsciousness. When next she awoke it was with the tongue of a beast licking her face, and a hairy body crouched against hers.

She started away with a cry. The beast beside her growled. Then she saw a segment of the darkness faintly sprayed with light, and dived for it. The beast did the same. Tangled, they scrambled out and looked at each other.

It was the wolf.

The morning was coming over mounded Windsor. Far up the attenuated Thames a snipe was calling. The air was clean and sweet with the night-time rain. Gay Hunter picked herself up from the grass and leaned against the side of the mound and wept for a little, watched by the bright eyes of the wolf. Then she saw that his chest and forepaws were matted with mould, and realised what had happened.

'If you won't bite me, I'd like to hug you. In fact, even if you do.'

The wolf submitted, shyly, again licking her so that it

45

tickled. Gay rubbed the spot and laughed, hugging him closer.

'Alive, really alive. Oh, goodness, and just because you followed me! There was never quite a morning like this before, or air like this, or a nice furry face like yours – or anyone so good to look at as I am, was there, Towser? Come on, I'll race you.'

When she sank down panting and exhausted, the Windsor mounds were in the south; in the east the fires of the great saucer were dim and fading in the morning light, but, barring progress in that direction, there arose to view now, with purple heads bright in the morning light, a great brake of giant thistles. They towered to a height of twenty feet, high and still in the air that was sweet with the smell of them, for they were in flower. Rabbits lolloped on the edge of the brake and the new-christened Towser growled carnivorously at sight of them. No other beast or human being was in sight.

Houghton?

Lady Jane Easterling?

They had vanished as completely as though swallowed by the storm. Gay went down to the reed-fringed Thames and lay and drank water there.

The wolf drank beside her, and she saw their joint images reflected back in the water, shakenly, from the little eddies that drifted from their mouths.

Lost! She was lost and alone in a deserted England, naked, in company with a lone wolf.

v

Famished and weak that afternoon, she and the wolf came on the great herds of wild pig.

They were grunting and rootling and squealing in the groves of a stone-oak wood. The ground was thick with their droppings and thick with acorns, and the air almost equally thick with their smell. It smelt like a Chesterton-delighting congress of the genus Pig. The nearer brutes hardly roused at all at the approach of Gay and the wolf. Evidently wolves did not hunt pigs. Towser sniffed warily, wurred, and gave

46

them a wide berth. It was Gay now who felt carnivorous.
'If only I had a decent butcher's equipment. . . . '

She might as well long for a Lewis gun. The porkers
grunted as they passed up the forest aisles. Gay picked some
acorns and tried to eat them, finding them tough enough fare.
The pigs were not the beasts of piggeries and sties of Mexico
or Milwaukee, but hairy and athletic-looking specimens,
guarded here and there by great boars. One of these, with
wart-like obtrusions on his nose, rose from a pleasant
mud-slough as Gay and the wolf passed and screamed at
them. Gay looked back. The boar was sharpening his tusks
on the ground. That operation completed, he launched
himself, galumphing, in pursuit.

Gay took to a tree, scraping her skin as she fled into the
higher branches. The boar had neglected to learn
tree-climbing in his youth and panted and screamed
disappointedly around the trunk. None of the rest of the
swine paid any heed. Gay imagined Towser had deserted her,
but next minute saw him worrying at the boar's heels. The
boar turned round, eager for battle.

It was an ungenteel and odoriferous encounter. When Gay
slipped down at last the great boar, minus its throat, was
slobbering out its life on the ground. The wolf fell twice and
then pulled itself up to its feet and, standing gingerly, began to
lick its wounds. The pigs rooted and grunted around,
undisturbed. Gay, very weak, sat down beside Towser and
cleansed his wounds while he snarled at her apologetically.

Then they both turned towards the dead boar.

vi

Moving restlessly in stomach-ache that night on the
outskirts on the stone-oak forest, she heard Towser also
moving. Raw boar was having as uneasy a reception in his
interior as in hers. She rubbed him consolingly, and he licked
her. It was near morning.

Early in the dawn light she saw a line of hills come
marching down from the north.

47

5. Rain in the Chilterns

i

THEY WERE the Chilterns. By noon that day she was deep in the grassy midst of them. In those desolate hills no birds sang, though once she and Towser paused to watch a great condor sweep overhead. Towser snarled and crouched close to the ground.

'Looking for other game,' said Gay. 'I think these are the Chiltern Hundreds. Where do we go from here?'

Her voice sounded strange in that silent land. Sometimes the warning would come to her, if this should go on — on and on — she would become insane. She sat down and considered it while the sunlight drowsed down upon her brown back and bent head. Supposing she were the last human being left alive? There had been no sign of any in all the journey from Pewsey — apart from the mummified cadaver of Windsor. None anywhere. The human race might have passed from the earth. And she might go on wandering these hills and llanos for months, years yet, never see a human face or hear a human voice, till madness and death came on her and she too passed. Why try to live at all?

She spoke again, aloud, to herself, to Towser: 'I think I know the answer to that. Though it's only half an answer, and half a lie, and I'm saying it to console myself. The answer's just — try and think it in words so that you won't go mad next minute — because it's nice to go naked and be yourself, not anyone else. Nice to have the scuff of the skin of your legs against one another. Nice to have nice breasts like mine in the sunlight. And watch the blood in your hand. And be free. And the fun of lying down and standing up and going there and coming hither without a single article to carry — without owning a thing in the world. And the goodness of that raw pig I ate last night, and the taste of water out of a stream with a throat really parched. And squatting in grass and watching the moon, though I'm so damnably frightened of panthers. Because of all that. A Testament to Life. And I've pinched some from the King's Canary, dear old Bridges. . . . But . . . '

But, even so, if there were no objective to her wanderings? Then there strayed through her mind again that fragment of a nursery rhyme Nurse Geddes would sing down in Mexico when she was a baby:

> *'Gay go up, and Gay go down:*
> *That is the way to London Town!'*

She must try and get out of these hills and make London. It couldn't be more than thirty or so miles away, London — or the place where London had been. She rubbed her aching feet. Perhaps with a stick — what a fool she had been not to gather herself a staff back there in the oak forest!

She stood up and Towser did the same. He was getting tamer, though still independent. And suddenly it came on Gay with a shock of realisation that made her almost sick with gladness, that she couldn't be the last human being after all. Some were left, some still sufficiently like her in kind to tame wolves to their service as dogs. Else Towser would never have behaved as he had done. He must have been someone's dog — somewhere.

Sure? She looked again at him. He had little of the dog about him. Was it just a freak chance that he had adopted her, as the she-wolf Romulus and Remus? If he had had a master, why had she seen no signs of human beings?

'I give it up, Towser. Ever see anyone like me before?'

He cocked his normal ear at her, then looked away, mildly bored. As she got to her feet he also stood up, but stiffly. The wounds from the fight in the pig-forest still troubled him. Gay patted his head, and the two of them limped on again.

To-morrow they would turn south-east.

Next morning when she awoke the wolf had disappeared. She called and called from the hollow where she had lain down with him beside her, but he did not return. She climbed up in the dew of the morning to look from the summit of a hill, and so saw the Chilterns spread out before her, rolling in undulation like an outline map. South was the glimmer of the great volcanic fire, north a mantling of dark green upon the horizon that was doubtlessly another forest. East was a shimmer of mist the sun was driving before it out of the low country of Thames-side. Into the west was a land of shadows, a land of grassy llanos.

'Towser!'

She searched till she found a pool, and squatted and drank and then set out eastwards, very hungry. As the day rose so did the heat. Her head began to ache in sympathy with her feet. Then she came on a great stretch of moor covered with blueberries. She knelt down and gathered them and stuffed them in her mouth in a passion of hunger, the acrid taste of them more lovely than anything else she had ever known. Eating, she heard a scuffle in the grass and, looking round, she promptly had her face licked by Towser. Tasting the blueberry juice on her face he sneezed. Gay had her arms around his neck, scolding him, when she was aware of being watched by other eyes. She turned her head.

He was halted at a distance of six feet or so away. He leaned on his unstrung bow. He was about Gay's own height but even slimmer, his skin much darker. He had a girdle with two arrows and a knife in it. Otherwise he was as naked as herself. She raised staring eyes to his face.

It was a young face, a haunting face, friendly and puzzled, with a broad brow and the downy beginning of a beard. The hair was hacked short in front and ended in a bang behind. His lips were full and red, startlingly red in the brown face. He might have been her own age or a little more.

Gay said, in a still, quiet voice: 'Who are you?'

The broad brow under the short-cut hair wrinkled in puzzlement. Then he said, very slowly and haltingly, as one speaking an alien speech:

'I am Rem. Wolf was my dog. But he went away. Then he came back last night and has led me here.'

'I'll cry in a minute. Please, am I mad? Are you really human? And — English, speaking in English — you can't! Or what century is it, what's happening to the world?'

He shook his head. Then he let the bow drop and squatted down in the grass. She had a sudden thrill of fear. He said, 'I do not understand. Only the dying Voices speak this speech. And they grow fainter every hunting season as we come back to the Place of Voices. The Old Singer says that when he was young the Voices were still very loud. None care to listen to them now. But I.'

Gay nodded. 'I see. Voices. And they're growing fainter. I've a fellow-feeling for them. . . . What do we do now?'

He looked at her, puzzled. She saw the startling breadth of the space between his eyes. He said, uncertainly:

'Do?'

Gay nodded. 'Am I your prisoner? Where are you going to take me?'

He said, 'Prisoner?' and sat and thought, squatted dark-brown and still, like a figure from the caves of Ajanta. But suddenly it came on Gay that he was like no man she had ever seen. He was not merely a man of her century, naked, and browned by the sun: he was someone completely alien — in gesture and notion and the look in his eyes, with a body strange in control and movement. He said 'Prisoner?' again in the high, rather singing voice in which he had spoken — the accentuation of one with unfamiliar speech. Gay said, shakingly:

'Yes. Want it plainer? You're a man. You're a savage. You're stronger than I am, I suppose. Am I going to be taken and raped? Or eaten?'

He gave it up. Apparently he found her entirely incomprehensible. He said, 'I do not know where you are going. The Folk'— he waved a vague arm north-eastward into the Chilterns — 'are there.'

Gay stood up. 'Then for goodness' sake let's look them up.'

He stood up beside her. He was two or three inches taller. He smiled and put out a hand on her arm. Gay stiffened and then set her teeth. Here was where things began to happen. . . .

A moment later she broke away from him, panting. Her skin was tingling. It had felt as though an electric dynamo were stroking her. Yet he had been inoffensive enough. His brow wrinkled again at her jump. Gay said, stammeringly:

'I hate — being pawed. Always have done. Well, are you coming?'

iii

They halted at noon in a grassy dip a mile or so south of the new forest that Gay had seen on the northwards skyline. Gay sat and watched him make a fire to cook the great bird, like a turkey, he had shot with his bow an hour or so before. It was quiet and still in the midsummer heat. Towser squatted panting: Rem's skin glistened as he knelt with a flint and a piece of iron pyrite brought from his girdle. He gathered dry grass and struck and struck the two instruments together till a spark was conceived and gave birth to a smoulder. Then he blew on it and gathered dried gorse-bush roots scattered around, and so made his fire. He did not speak. He had spoken hardly at all in their northwards tramp through the Chilterns. Gay lay back on the ground with her hands under her head and watched him, in drowsy appraisal.

So this was how it had all ended: all the great things of that century out of which she had come, all the skill with machine and tool, the giant bridges and the great furnaces, the airships that clove the sky, the silent, gigantic laboratories, the dreams and plans and hopes — ended in a naked savage with a flint and steel lighting a fire to cook his food amidst the ruin of a desolate England! All the futures that twentieth century had envisaged had been but dreams — collapse, and a return to savagery the outcome.

That Rem was a stray, a freak, she did not believe for a moment. He had the mark upon him of one of a recognised and acknowledged community. So much indeed she had gathered from his words — a community of hunters who came south with the summer and in winter went north

52

into some waste where another Great Fire lighted the sky perpetually. The England of Shakespeare, Newton, Avebury — it had ended in nakedness, brown skins, and a bow. . . .

Towser thrust his nose against her, questioningly. She patted his head, and lay still in the sunlight, an arm around his neck. You could not be sad long in this flare of sunlight, over a battle lost long ago. Suddenly you realised how tired you were — sleepy and tired. Till that bird had cooked. . . .

She was shaken awake by Rem. The bird was ready. She awoke sun-tired and blinked drowsy eyes. They sat side by side, the three of them, and ate the unauthentic turkey while the sun wheeled over to afternoon. Then Rem wiped his fingers on the grass and picked up his bow. It was time to go.

But south of the forest they came on a great stretch of heath, growing a plant that seemed to Gay faintly recognisable. Then she saw that wild hogs had been here, rootling in the earth, and that the waste stretch of giant weeds was a great potato-patch. Tubers lay round. She pointed to them.

'They are good to eat.'

The hunter halted and looked at them, then shook his head.

'They kill — here, so close to the Great Fire. They began to kill in the days of the Voices.'

'Kill? Poisonous?'

'They are not good. They kill.'

Gay knelt and scooped one from the ground and broke it open. She found it a strange potato. It had developed a core. The core was a dull red hardness. Strange transformation of the potato! Poison. Poisoned potatoes. How? How long ago?

Impossible to know. Impossible perhaps ever to know. She glanced up at the brown flanks of Rem and found his eyes upon her. He smiled — bearded, a strange, alien boy, and Gay found herself smile in return. For a minute she knelt there among the poisoned potatoes, smiling at him in the sunlight. Then he put out his hand and slowly she put hers into his. Something dim and symbolical as he raised her from amidst the evil tubers of an hebetic past. . . . He turned towards the forest.

She left her hand in his. Footsore though she was, she was aware of a sudden lightness. Oh, what did it matter,

53

that time long past? How much had anyone lost when that battle was lost? Why, in this dead England even your toes — dead things; Lord, how dead things toes had been! — began to live, to thrill and be suddenly in harmony with the life in the grass they pressed, in the flare of the sun. As though all your life you have been a living mind in the body of a corpse, till that accident of a neo-Dunne night!

They had come to the straggling beginnings of the trees. The fingers dropped away from hers. With their doing so, her tiredness came back, queerly. He was a helpful boy, if only he would say a little more. What now?

He glanced at her and then at the trees. She also looked over their crests. Fleecy masses of clouds, not the great thunder-clouds that had caught her at Windsor, but masses like carded wool, were rolling down from the north. With their coming came a chill in the wind. The forest shoomed and murmured. Rem beckoned her to follow him and turned sideways, skirting the trees.

So it was she came to the chalk cliff that verged upon that oak forest — it seemed as though its end had been carved abruptly away, as though at the stroke of a great axe. It fronted westward and mosses faced the chalk here and there, its face was crumbling and ancient. But as they drew nearer Gay saw that her imagining had been more than imagining. Other agencies than those of wind and rain had once played upon this rock. She paused below it and put up her hands to shade her eyes, remembering those pictures carved by Darius in commemoration of his victories on the rock of Behistun.

The figures had been deeply incised into the face of the cliff, and then, perhaps, the incisions faced with some staying acid, for the incisions were a dark green, as through a spreading stain. Yet, even so, many thousands of years must have passed since the sculptor carved those figures, for they were half overlaid by the rain-drip of the chalk, though the cliff-brow itself served as a shielding overhang. Time had stroked them with countless hands and would yet obliterate them. So doing, it would obliterate perhaps the foulest thing ever emerged from the diseased mind of men.

Gay lowered her eyes, in a sickened shame. The beauty of the human body she knew, its ugliness as well, the beauty and

54

ugliness of love and lust she had read of, talked of, if never herself endured. Sometimes she had envisaged them as mighty adventures awaiting her in the future — thrilling and terrible and tremendous, the lust as the love. They were the ultimate and lovely mystery, she had thought, gay little materialist, seeing all mystic philosophies and hopes as the play of diseased reflexes only, the wind and gusty regurgitation of human life. And all the world, whatever the names and sickened stomachic dreamings of gods and heavens and hells and codes they had shielded behind, had believed with her in the tremendousness of lust and love. Even this sculptor had believed.

But he had made of them a foulness and a Satanic abomination on this cliff-face. Centuries ago. In an agony of hate and disgust he had portrayed them.... It was hate, hate insane and dreadful, from which Gay turned shamed eyes. The power and the sickening beauty of the thing would etch a reproduction in her mind for ever, she thought. She — she who had been so liberal and so unshamed in everything – she did not dare lift her eyes to Rem.

Till his silence grew unendurable. Then she looked up, slowly. He was looking not at the sculpture, but at her, the same ghost of a waiting smile upon his lips, awaiting hers. He had discovered her smile and was waiting for it to come back. It did not. Instead, Gay seized his arm. She thought, 'I must look like one tingling blush, but this has to be settled for good.' She pointed up at the dreadful caricature on the cliff-brow.

'Look! That picture. What do you think of it — you and your people?'

His eyes followed the direction in which she pointed. She watched him. He looked puzzled. He said, 'Picture? I do not see a reflection.'

'But in front of us — up there, on the cliff!'

Only at the end of a minute's gesticulation did she realise the truth. For him the picture did not exist. It was a mere scrawling and indenting upon the face of the cliff. It had for him no relevance at all, human, divine, or demoniac.

iv

They camped under the Horror. The rain had come on —
long, wavering pelts that fled over the brow of the cliff into
the space where the firs stood with bayonets to receive the
flying charges of the rain-cavalry. Gay padded about
collecting wood and feeding the fire that Rem had made,
pausing now and again to watch that combat of tree and rain.
Now with the rising of the wind and the sinking of the sun a
red smoulder over the tundra, the voice of the trees rose,
strumming and hesitant at first, but with deep under-notes
that played one upon the other and mounted and mounted,
as though seeking some final tremendous rhythm. There was
no sign of Rem. He had gestured to her to heed to the fire and
had vanished into the forest with Towser.

Gay's short hair streamed about her head. She felt no cold
—her body was becoming attuned to the blow of wind and
the flare of sun alternately. Her hands, rested upon her hips
(she suddenly realised the attitude), seemed so much part of
her body there she had had no consciousness of attitude. She
put up her hand through her hair and heard it crackle as with
electricity. Lovely shampoo. . . .

'And I'm hungry. I hope he brings back a young elephant.'

He brought back instead eggs, great pheasant's eggs, and
his girdle full of plums. Towser came shooting in advance
seeking the shelter of the cliff. The hunter's brown body was
pelted by the stinging rain-drops as he ran for the fireside —
the water coursed from him in a little spray. Then he and Gay
stood and smiled at each other, till she suddenly remembered
that thing carved upon the cliff above them, and her face
froze. Silly, but she couldn't help it.

He said, slowly and carefully: 'We will cook the eggs and
eat them.'

Gay looked round. 'But where's your skillet?'

He shook his head, gave up the unknown word, and knelt
down to scrape a hole under the fire. Into this he laid the eggs
and dragged a light coating of earth over them. Gay thought:
'They'll probably crack, and we'll have to eat them with earth
as salt. But he ought to know what he's doing. . . . Hell 'n' blast,
I'm going to have a shower-bath as well!'

56

She ran out into the pelt of the rain. As she did so the sun shone and wheeled on her for a moment, pelted by the flying raindrops. Rem stared. Towser stared. All the Chilterns stopped to stare, entertained.

She ran back into the shelter of the defaced cliff-side and sank down by the fire to dry herself. Rem squatted cross-legged at the other side. Towser sniffed and lay down, his nose pointed towards the fire. They awaited the eggs. Suddenly the unreality of it touched Gay, fleetingly, only a moment, yet as with a frozen wing-tip. Herself, Gay Hunter of New York and Mexico City, seated naked here under an English cliffside, in a ruined and abandoned England, in the company of a naked savage and a wolf! And seated — to an onlooker it would have looked like a family group in the beginnings of the world.

Beastly, that, as Mother would have said. And yet, why? He looked a nice boy, and cuddlesome, if it wasn't for that feeling of unreality that came upon you in the oddest of moments in his presence. Some dragging maladjustment of the time-space continuum — the thought and the knowledge that when you were growing up a young woman in Mexico of the twentieth century that curved, beautiful body there was not even seed in a womb, seed in the womb of any woman for thousands of years to come. That knowledge it was dragged upon your eyelids and your brain every now and then. . . .

Dimly she remembered out of a far gulf the singing of a poet:

> 'Our birth is but a sleep and a forgetting;
> The soul that rises with us, our life's star,
> Hath had elsewhere its setting,
> And cometh from afar;
> Not in entire forgetfulness,
> And not in utter nakedness,
> But trailing clouds of glory do we come
> From God, who is our home:
> Heaven lies about us in our infancy!'

Poor Wordsworth! Great Wordsworth! But he'd never envisaged a scene like this. How very shocked he'd have

57

been — after his French days, at least. The boughs on the fire gave a crackling noise and fell in, and Gay started from her dream. Rem bent forward and raked away the embers and was picking out hot eggs and handing them to her. His skin seemed capable of withstanding any degree of temperature. Gay's was less well inured. She dropped the egg and blew upon her fingers.

'Idiot!'

He looked puzzled again, then smiled. He did more than that. He chuckled gravely. Suddenly the full humour of it came upon him. He lay on the ground and wept with laughter. Gay stared an astounded resentment, and then laughed herself. It was very contagious. Towser growled, laughing. There was not a humorous thing within miles, but they laughed till they were tired. Then Rem was as suddenly serious again, cracking off the shells of the eggs and eating them by the simple expedient of popping them one by one into his mouth. Around rose the desolate Chilterns, under their garment of rain.

Near sunset that rain cleared. Gay, for urgent and personal reasons, abandoned the hunter and climbed up and around the cliff, motioning Rem not to follow. He said, 'Yes,' and nodded. The elementary decencies still survived. Under her feet the grass was wet, yet warm, tickling her live toes as she ran up the hill. Here were bushes, gorse, and some berry bushes she had never seen before. All the sky was banded greatly in amber. She sat down and looked over the forest to more hills beyond, and then west into the far llanos that shrouded the ancient England from the sight of the sun, far down under mould and humus and the dust of the years. It was very quiet, the sunset quiet.

She put her hands up before her eyes to look in that colourful silence. As she did so, a cricket began to chirp, quite near at first it seemed, then receding, the little beast hopping away, exploratory, into the west. More clouds were coming from the north, but for a little the sunset's colour resisted them, and the lost girl waited and watched that deepening tinting of the Western sky — food-filled, and contented, filled with a macabre sadness as well. And she remembered other sadnesses, those passing sadnesses of adolescence, from which her father had been wont to rouse her in Mexico with sardonic jollity. If only this were the sadness of adolescence, this sadness for a world that had passed.

And in a sudden vision, as though torn from a kinematographic reel, she saw the lines of faces in Broadway of a night, in the Strand of a night, down the white Boul' Mich., down Plaza Nacional, and dimly backgrounding those dim hosts the great buildings and lights of their time. So strong they had seemed, enduring for ever, built of the blood and sweat of the hosts, outlasting centuries. And it had been no more than a seeming. How had they all ended and passed? (For she was sure they had passed.) And how long ago? Would she ever find out? Perhaps the Voices that Rem talked about would help her. . . .

And herself?

O God, she had not thought about herself!

She might live for fifty or sixty years yet — *how*? Roaming the countryside with a wolf, eating fruit, climbing trees — she would go mad! Life an eternal picnic — it was the kind of thing that sick little imaginative novelists had dreamt of in the smoke and squalor and the unemployment queues of the fourth decade of the twentieth century. But how impossible — for life — in any life. Yet, what else was there here, what else could she do?

And a sudden panic coming upon her at that thought, she jumped to her feet and ran down the cliff to the side of the fire where Rem was squatting. He jumped up at the haste of her approach, looking over her shoulder and snatching at his bow. She beat on his chest with demented fists.

'No, no. Not that! There's nothing after me. But — how am I to live, what am I to do? What do you ever do? Hunt and rest and eat and sleep — I'd go mad. We did other things long ago! I come from long ago, I tell you! Thousands of things, you hear!'

He stepped back a little, bewildered. Gay's hands dropped. She was weeping. The hunter understood tears. He took her in his arms. . . .

A moment later she shook herself free.

'Oh, damn! This is ridiculous — crying on the shoulder of a naked savage — crooning at me, too, instead of rape and

59

cannibalism and all the good story-book things . . . I wish — I wish handkerchiefs at least had survived.'

But they hadn't. She wiped her face, grubbily, with her hands and sat down. The wolf, Towser, came and snuffled and thrust his face in between breast and thigh, and snuffled again, consolingly. Rem had squatted down again, his hands clasped behind his head. It was nearly dark.

The rain whispered, coming on again. Looking over her shoulder, Gay saw its grey pelt pass over the trees to the grass-lands beyond — *The empty pastures blind with rain*, as someone had written of just such a scene. The night was now quite near, and in the closing in of the shadows the fire-glow ran up the face of the cliff and flickered on the filthy masterpiece of an aberrant genius — flickering it into an insane and monstrous life a moment, so that it spewed its foulness upon the forest. Gay lowered her eyes and looked at Rem, found him watching her with half-closed eyes. Of what was he thinking?

'What speech do you speak — not the one from the Voices that I am speaking — but your usual one?'

He thought this over for a little while. Then: 'The Tongue of the Folk.'

'Say some.'

He said some, crooning it, some song, perhaps. It sounded strange to Gay's ears, yet with a vague, far trace of familiarity here and there. She began to question the hunter as the darkness deepened around them, comparing word for word the English speech for grass and trees and wolf with that which the Folk spoke. There could be no doubt — the hunter spoke a simple agglutinative tongue, without tense or time, such tongue as the Europe of her day had long abandoned. Where had it come from? Whence the ancestors of Rem himself?

She asked him that, but he did not know. They trod dimly on the fringe of an uncertain understanding a while, and then desisted. She asked him where the Place of the Voices was, and he raised himself on an elbow to point north of the dripping forest.

Gay questioned that gesture with upraised eyebrows: 'To-morrow?'

'Perhaps to-morrow.'

Perhaps to-morrow. She looked up at the sculptured filthiness. Would the Voices tell her anything of that or the times that had made it? And what were those Voices? Dying Voices? . . . Useless puzzling. She found that she was very sleepy. So was Towser. He had appropriated the best place in front of the fire. She nudged him to move, and he did so with a sleepy, dissatisfied grunt. Oh God, what fun to sleep on a mattress again!

Gay lay down and curled herself almost like the wolf. Rem squatted staring into the fire — strange figure there, like a figure from some Early Egyptian relief. Something ached in her heart, looking at him — a kind of aching wonder, a desire. Then she closed that away, with sleep pressing her eyelids. She called:

'Good night.'

He said, 'It will rain all night,' after a glance at the sky.

v

It did more than that. Sometime in the night the wind veered several points. Gay woke in the stinging pelt of ice-cold rain and for a time was horribly confused as to place and circumstance, and crawled half-erect and stared at the fire. It was dying to a low smoulder. Over in the shelter, directly under the lee of the cliff, the hunter and the wolf were sleeping side by side. As she moved erect the wolf snarled and then, recognising her, lowered his head. Gay poked the fire and, dripping, ran in under that shelter.

Here it was dry and warm, with the firelight flinging a dull glow on the stretched bodies of Rem and his wolf. The space was narrow and she crouched back against the wall. As she did so a hand came out of the half-darkness upon her leg, closing around it.

It made her heart jump. Then she saw the hunter was awake. He made unmistakable motions: she should lie between him and the wolf.

A long moment Gay stood and looked down at him,

61

seeing this moment and its chances so clearly, seeing this adventure to which she gave herself. Then sleep brought down its veils, obliterating heroism and risk and regret. She slipped down between hunter and wolf, thrusting her long legs towards the fire. For a moment she lay rigid, and then turned her head towards the hunter.

He put an arm across her, a sleep-warm arm. The fine hair on it tickled her skin to a sudden thrill. She bit her lips, sleepily panic-stricken. All right. If only he would get on with the business. . . .

The arm did not move. She glanced at his face in the flicker of the firelight.

He was fast asleep.

For a minute the relief of that drove sleep from her eyes. Then a wonder came on her, a whimsical dismay. Was she as bad as that — funny and brown, Lady Jane had called her? So bad that a savage on a raining night refused to play the fitting rôle to which any pornographic novelist would have assigned him? And she had thought she would be rather sweet to sleep with!

Then she saw the blue shadows under the hunter's eyes. He was dead tired. They were alive — in a life real at least, in a life, it seemed, where you slept at least, fully and completely. Probably loved in like manner — breath-taking thing to think of, that!

The arm was heavy, but warm upon her. She put up her hand to that relaxed hand and gave it a little squeeze. The hunter turned away from her, still in sleep.

Blessed boy.

She cuddled closer to him at that, a hand upon his warm hip. He had a nice and seemly and well-shaped hip. Her own fingers relaxed. She fell asleep.

6. The Dam

i

WHEN GAY awoke on a morning three days later, she found herself surrounded by a score or so of naked brown bowmen.

In the space of those three days she and the hunter and Towser the wolf had wandered a slow way in and out through the Chilterns. Early on the morning of the first day they had come to a great stagnant lake, and as they bathed in it there arose near Gay a beast like a tiger, it seemed to her. It was a giant otter. It had snarled at her, terrifyingly, while Rem shouted and made towards the scene with loud splashings. So close had it risen that its soft coat had almost brushed Gay's arm. She had dived. So had the otter. Fortunately they took opposite directions, and fortunately made for opposite banks, leaving Rem and Towser to follow more slowly.

'What a damnable beast!' Gay had said, wiping water from herself with her hands. 'Are there many like that?'

A reminiscent look had come into the hunter's eyes. 'There are the great dogs of the north,' he had said, and tried, unambitiously, to tell her of their great-maned ferocity. Gay had wrinkled a puzzled brow at him. Lions? Could they be lions?

At noon they had come on a strawberry paradise. Great strawberries rioted and throve despite the clinging waste of weeds. The hunter and Gay sat and ate like — like the greediest of children, she thought, wiping her stained mouth as she stood erect again in the flare of the sunshine. The sunshine was much warmer than once it had been, she noted. Was the sun larger — or nearer? It seemed the same to her hand-shaded eyes. But what a summer!

Yet, that day and the next, she made notchings of calculations on a stick she now carried — marking the notches with a stone. The days were short — definitely shorter

63

than once they had been. Some great change had smitten the earth since the days when she drove the hired Morgan up through the Wiltshire Downs. Perhaps the men of the ages between had actually succeeded in righting the poles — setting the earth upright, so to speak — before disaster overtook them.

What had that been? How? Useless question!

Then she remembered how in her own far time the earth was said to be still but slowly recovering from the effects of the Fourth Glacial Age. Perhaps this was the midst of the heyday that had awaited her times. The earth had grown a great sunshine garden again, yet with no such increase of moisture as to bring back the tropic jungles. And that mighty civilisation that might have so gloried and adventured in this Arcady had vanished away and was not even a dim remembrance.

For Rem knew little or nothing of it — or would tell her nothing. He would tell her little of even the Voices from which he had learned his English — he had learned it according to some formula orally preserved in the bardic traditions of his Folk — and equated it with meanings in his own agglutinative tongue. But he told that this habit of heeding to the Voices was dying out, even as the Voices themselves were dying. Gay asked why, and he said because the Folk had tired of the Voices. . . . They were just a foolish crying in the dark.

He told her that the second night of their camping, in the midst of a great cane-brake, the fire crackling and spluttering as they fed it idly with cane-joints. 'It was some unhappy time that came on the Folk long ago,' he amplified. 'When Great Beasts killed them and they themselves were mad. So are the Voices mad. But they pass, and we endure.'

He said it in his low sing-song, and abandoned the subject, stretching out a hand instead to stroke Gay's leg. He liked doing that, not shyly, or impertinently, or desirously. Half-wittedly, rather, Gay had thought at first, with a touch of impatience. But now she was less sure. He seemed rather to do it with a concentrated enjoyment of the sensation of touch of which her own blunted nerve-instruments were incapable. Standing on the verge herself, she glimpsed for him a

64

passionate enjoyment of such things, exquisitely sensuous as great music to the peoples of her time. He was not the blank-minded child she had once thought. Instead....

She put down her hand on the hand on her leg. 'Sometime you'll tell me all about how to live. I'd love to know!'

He lay still, his hand still on her leg and his eyes remote. Didn't he ever want to sleep with her, Gay thought, sleepily? Should she tempt him and see?

It would have been very easy in the ancient world. She thought of all the technique of display and coquetry and attraction in use among the women of her time. Hell 'n' blast, what a waste of life it had all been! — the jewels, the henna'ed finger-nails, the frou-frou of silken skirts, the leprosy-powdered faces, the stained lips — all for the purpose of attracting a male to the supreme purpose of fertilising the female! Yet thousands of those women who had dressed and painted and ogled had done so with a dispassionate calculation, giving their favours for substantial returns, or perhaps giving them never at all, carrying on the maddening technique with no thought of ever bringing the act to fruition. ... Beasts. Goodness, those must have been the Great Beasts of whom Rem's folk had their tradition!

She had looked up from the cane-brake to see the stars bright and unclouded that night, marching their hosts east, strange hosts in a strange sky. Where was she herself being led — where could she ultimately go? And automatically the jingle from nursery days answered her:

> 'Gay go up and Gay go down:
> That is the way to London Town!'

If there were a London — as Houghton and Lady Jane had so passionately believed. What had happened to those two — dead or astray like herself? She squeezed that hand on her leg.

'You were a dear to find me — you and Towser.'

He said something in his own language that she could not comprehend. His eyes questioned hers, lightedly. She shook her head.

'You may be questioning my age, my religion — you know my sex — or my taste in light literature. I don't know. Or my name. I never told you my name.'

65

He said, 'What is your name?'

'Gay Hunter.'

It was only as she said it that, for the first time in her life, she recognised the barbaric quality of her name. Here, in this milieu, it might sound no more than a descriptive nickname. And in that sense, indeed, it was obvious that Rem took it.

'It is a good name,' he said in his accentless sing-song. 'You are the Gay Hunter and I am Rem — the Singer.'

'So that's what it means. Singer? Sing some now, then.'

He shook his head. 'I sing for the Folk.'

So that was that. No sociabilities. She pushed his hand away fearlessly and curled up, enjoyably, to sleep — without bed, blankets, sheets, or (she thought, drowsily) a care in the world.

ii

Then, wakening, she found the hunters round about her. They had trooped in with the dawn-light, drawn by the smell of Rem's fire in the cane-brake. A score or so in number they squatted on the ground, a circle of savages watching Gay Hunter awake, with that owlish, malignant stupidity of the savage in their gestures and look. Slowly the light grew stronger as Gay lay with bated breath and watched the circle. Then she saw the faces more clearly. With the passing of the last of the night, the last of her fears, foul-born in that age out of which she had come, went by as well. She sat up and shook the dew from her hair. Rem and the wolf, after a first glance at the savage newcomers, had taken to sleep again.

Savage?

They were just a collection of brown-skinned hunters, quite naked, tired from a night's hunting (one carried a pig, and several carried birds), waiting for the courtesies of a fire and welcome.

She got up and poked the fire. The circle did not move. Dried thorn-canes lay around, and she fed the grey ashes, kneeling to blow upon them. All the air was fresh and keen, alive with a twittering of birds. As she lay full-length upon the ground and blew at the ashes, she felt a hand upon her,

66

and for a moment, as with Rem, lay rigid. Then she turned round slowly and looked at the hunter. He smiled and yawned, stretching his arms elaborately. (He was *shy!*)

They began to speak among themselves, not loudly — in order not to disturb Rem, Gay guessed. She could make nothing of the long, agglutinative roll of speech. Some words seemed to be addressed to her, and she shook her small dolichocephalic head at the brachycephalic heads of the hunters. Most of them seemed neither young nor old, of medium height, berry-brown, long-legged, with little body hair, but clustering bangs of brown and black hair about their heads. Some were stained and splashed, as though from hunting through fords or rivers. One had a missing hand that made her shudder, so crudely had it been doctored. They had low, broad foreheads and eyes like Rem's, the eyes of people hardly individualised in the sense that the twentieth century had understood individuation. They were impossible, but they were real enough, this group of folk into which time and a fantastic accident had brought her.

She tried English on them: 'We've no food, and I'm hungry. Shall we cook the pig?'

Such of those as were not dozing looked from one to the other with sleepy, questioning eyes. Evidently Rem was almost the only one who had the speech of the Voices. But at her gesture one of them understood. He came forward and began to dig a pit in the earth to roast the pig, much as Rem had done earlier with the eggs. Gay, pressed by elementary needs, took herself out of the encirclement and went down through an opening in the cane-brake. She heard the scuff of feet behind her, and looked round and saw a young, bronzed figure following.

'Go away!'

He grinned, shyly, and went. Gay resumed her course through the brake, her breath a little quicker. Though she felt inclined to laugh. If Rem were slow, there seemed others who were speedy enough. . . .

When she came back Rem was awake and the encampment astir with a hum of voices. The singing of the birds in the brake was blindingly sweet. Some of the hunters were lying on their backs, listening to it. One was mending a bow. But the most were engaged in answering a fire of questions from Rem. There was something exciting in the air, though it had not moved that dreaming speculation from Rem's eyes. At Gay's appearance the talk quietened. All stared.

She began to blush, angrily: then laughed. Rem's grave face broke into an answering smile. The encampment grinned and resumed its conversation. Her advent from the twentieth century had been accepted.

But there was apparently something else more difficult of acceptance. The pig, in an hour or so, was excavated and eaten. The impertinent young hunter who had shown an inclination to follow Gay earlier in the morning came and sat down beside her and hacked off a succulent piece of pork for her delectation. Gay took it on a leaf, and ate hungrily. Flirting had survived all else.

But now there was a movement to be afoot. Rem stamped out the fire and the hunters caught up their sparse gear. Rem led the way out of the brake and the others followed. Gay and the flirtatious hunter brought up the rear.

Where now?

iii

She received her answer before the coming of night. All day, hunting slowly and spreading out fanwise in the process, they loitered northwards, but evidently with a fixed enough objective. Once they roused a bear — a great creature at which two or three arrows were loosed. It snapped them off and charged the attackers. They scattered with yells, but closed in again about the beast. Gay, squeamishly, did not look on at the last incident. Rem joined her here.

'Where are we going?'

'To the Place — they want me at the Place.' His eyes wrinkled up, and he looked at her strangely. 'There are others.'

'What others?'

He shook his young, bearded head, uncommunicative as ever, and rejoined the hunt. For lunch Gay had a piece of warm bear meat, sweet and rich. Unfortunately, it made her sick. The sympathetic and flirtatious young hunter — his name was a wooden clatter of syllables: Allalalaka — insisted on coming with her behind the bush *to hold her head*!

Then, the party again in motion with the wearing of the afternoon, they came on the edge of the great Dam once excavated in the heart of the Chilterns by the antique men of a time that had yet been in the future of Gay's twentieth century.

She was never able to guess the purpose of that giant Dam or the interlocking maze of corridors and passages at its upper end in which the Folk now sheltered when they came hunting here in the summer. Perhaps it had been a new water reservoir for London. Perhaps to feed some other city now long dust and rubble. It had a dizzying depth, especially at the far end under the corridors, a width of four miles or so, and a length of perhaps five. Great boulders had rolled down on it from the sides of the hills. Heath and grass had encroached upon the floor of it, here and there. But it still endured to shape, though the feed at the head of its five miles stretch was broken and the once-prisoned waters long gone. Only midway of it now a shallow stream flowed and murmured, gradually wearing out a channel for itself, through a substance that seemed otherwise everlasting.

Standing above the Dam in company with the hunters, Gay gasped, thinking for a moment that here at least men must still be capable of great engineering feats. Then she saw the antiquity of the Dam. Had it been made of any kind of stone, even andesite or diorite, like the great ruins left by the pre-Inkans in Peru, it would long since have crumbled to dust. But, instead, it was made of metal.

No more than the purpose of the Dam, was she ever to discover the alloy of which that metal was made. There seemed to be copper in it, for, beyond the points and pilasters of the Dam, over the ruined passages and corridors that the Folk had made their shelters, there lifted up into the afternoon air, fragile, tremendous and lovely, a great tower some four hundred feet in height. Its upper reaches shone a dull green — the green of much-weathered copper, and bushes and then forest towered behind it. It was lonely, gigantic, terrifying, five miles away in the afternoon stillness.

Gay wondered what it could be, and sought out Rem.

'It is the Place of Voices.'

They scrambled down the slopes of the Dam till they reached the bottom, the strange metallic flooring of the great reservoir. In the air hung the blue smell of smoke. No herds were pastured in this secure hollow — she was to discover that the Folk knew nothing of, or cared nothing for, herds or tame cattle. Then, up at the broad end of the Dam, she saw fires winking as the evening came on.

It was almost dark before they reached those fires, glimmering in the bowels of the hills through the ruins of the Titanic metal masonry. Here stood great columns, of metal, imbedded straightly still in the dull metal floor of the Dam. Beyond showed the entrances, weather-smeared, but hardly weather-worn at all. And in those remote chambers, where perhaps once purifying chemicals had been stored to mix automatically with the waters, the hunter Folk had made their shelters, bringing there their weapons and fires and women and children, their slow, easy drift through summer days, their waning attention to the Voices of the Tower.... The flirtatious hunter, Allalalaka, helped Gay up over masses of metallic rubble to the mouth of one of the corridors.

Above its entrance was carved an inscription.

Suddenly Gay realised how old it was, how far off it was. She could make nothing of the script, except a faint letter here and there. It looped and wound, its secret lost in the technique of some alien writing.

She looked back over the deserted Dam, a wild pity holding her heart. Poor devils, poor people, those who had built this and dreamt of this, with no foreshadowing of the desolation their hands would make! A wild crying and running under the sun, under the moon, under the slow-changing stars, and civilisation had passed from men like a strange dream dreamed by a hunter's camp-fire, betwixt the time of his nodding and the low growl of his wolf-dog beside him, as some intruder trod in the night.

Young Allalalaka pulled at her hand.

Inside the ancient underground reservoir she found

some three or four hundred naked men and women and children, the smoke of their fires, and Lady Jane Easterling and Major Ledyard Houghton tied with thongs to an ancient metallic pillar from the floor.

7. Sunset

i

LYING ON the verge of sleep, she remembered the words she had spoken to Lady Jane:

'They'll probably cut your throats. I hope they do.'

'By God, you little bitch...' Houghton had said, strangledly.

She had turned away, leaving them hanging in their thongs, watched by the brown, wide-eyed hunters and their women. Some of the women as pretty as I am, Gay had thought, interestedly. Prettier even, confound them. And had smiled at one, very young and slim, with a whimsical thought about her:

'In the twentieth century, my dear, but for the grace of God and a father with a large income, they'd have covered over those nice knees and thighs of yours with wisps of clothing, and made you posture on a stage in a music hall — to excite scrubby little clerks into wonderment about what was under the clothes. Instead...'

Instead, she was as lovely as a deer. She smiled back at Gay. The flirtatious hunter came smiling as well. She gathered that she was invited to sit and eat roast pig. Only when they glanced to the bound twain by the pillar did something else come into their gay, dreamy eyes. Gay shivered. She had done nothing herself, and even were she in danger, she didn't think she'd shiver. . . . But Houghton and Lady Jane had probably only a short time to live.

From the babble of Lady Jane she had gathered little of what had happened till Houghton took to barking out his version in short, parade-ground sentences. . . . Windsor — that night — two of them caught in the rain. Came back in the morning — no sign of you, Miss Hunter — decided you must have gone on on your own. . . . So they set out themselves, and after four days' wandering fell in with some of those savages. Didn't try to attack, but it was a sickening business being in their hands, unarmed. Danger to Jane. So that night, while the hunters slept, Houghton had tried to steal their flint-tipped spears. Unfortunately, one of them had awakened and made a grasp at his spear. Lady Jane had crept behind him and smothered his face so that he couldn't cry, and then Houghton ... well, there had been nothing else for it. They had taken another spear and bow, and crept away from the camping-place, Houghton wiping the blood of the hunter from the original spear. Then they had made east, and camped, with no fire ... they couldn't make one though they wanted to. The savages must have tracked after them. They jumped on Houghton while he slept and tied him up, then Lady Jane, and drove them up through the wilderness to the edge of this Dam ... '

'And what are they going to do to us now? You seem to be friendly with them, Miss Hunter. My hands are hurting. Do get them to release us!'

This was Lady Jane. Gay had looked at her, in her tattered grass skirt and her filth-stained body, and suddenly had had a vision of that hunter killed by her and Houghton — one of these kindly, remote savages who had companioned herself. And it was then she had replied:

'I'm damned if I do. They'll probably cut your throats. I hope they do.'

Unkind enough, that, she thought now, turning uneasily on the nest of grass she shared with the naked, slim girl who had befriended her. Poor devils, she might have done something for them.... She peered through the eddying smoke. The fires were dying as the night wore on. From where she lay she could see Houghton and Lady Jane, still tied to the pillar. Lady Jane was sagging forward in her bonds.

Gay stood up and went in and out the fires till she stood beside them. Houghton whispered, hoarsely, 'She's fainted.'

Gay nodded, and looked round the great culvert. Overhead arched the roof of strange, green-crusted metal. In nests by the fires the hunters slept, men and women and naked, rosy-brown children. Yet they did not all sleep. She saw the firelight shine in eyes, regarding her, and for a moment had a trill of fear. Then that went past. She

73

went up to one of the fires and picked up a utensil from which she had seen them drink. It was no more than a twisted leaf — a leaf of some great plant she did not know. At the carved door of the culvert she hesitated, wondering how near water might be.

Out here, the night stung fresh and bright. Overhead was the glory of the stars. Very far off in the south some great beast was baying the moon — far off in the lower end of the great abandoned Dam. Listening for a minute or so she heard the gurgle of water, darkness-concealed, and made her way down towards that. It seemed a long distance. Once she fell and bruised her elbow and swore, and that helped, jerking the sleepiness from her eyes and mind. So at last she came to the edge of the stream that poured out of a circular metallic opening and meandered away through the quiet of the night and the bosom of the ruined land — with a sharp trilling it moved off into the darkness — *rejoicing, through the hushed Chorasmian waste,* said a stray phrase in her mind. She bent down and filled the leaf.

When she had attained to the great cave-culvert again, she splashed water in Lady Jane's face, and then gave her some to drink. Then she went again for water, this time for the parched Houghton.

He gulped and spluttered as the water went down his heat-dried throat. 'Very decent of you.'

'Rot. Any of these people would have done the same — if you hadn't started murdering amongst them first.'

'Don't lecture me, damn you. Filthy savages! By God, if I ever get loose among them — look here, they give you freedom enough, you could easily get me a knife.'

'And cut you loose — and get my own throat cut? No. thanks.'

They were speaking in whispers. Lady Jane joined in now. 'We could get away while they're asleep, and go down east again, on the road to London ... '

Gay drew a long breath. Hell 'n' blast, *would* they never learn? 'London? You think there's still a London — after seeing these people?'

'Of course there must be — some central place of authority.' This was Houghton. 'These are just animals — beasts.

74

I've seen sickening sights tonight! One of them with two women ...'

'There's no need to make me feel sick again, Ledyard. Can't you persuade this girl to get us away?'

Gay was angry by now. 'No, he can't persuade this girl, damn you. But I'll see what I can do with one of these hunters about you – he may plead for you. He speaks English.'

'What?' Houghton moved and pulled at his bonds. 'I thought as much. These are no more than some stray tribe of Gipsies. One of them knows English, eh? If we could get to London ...'

'You'd find it a place full of sea-gulls, most likely.... Good night.'

They whispered after her urgently, but she paid them no heed, going back to her grass couch by the side of the girl who was sleeping so soundly.

As Gay sank down beside her, she turned round and took Gay in her arms.

ii

When she woke the cave was deserted but for herself, the young girl, and Allalalaka. Into the mouth of the culvert poured the early sunshine. She heard the sound of far voices. There was the stench of much fire – burning and cooking in the air.

The girl – her name was Liu – had cooked pork for her, and Allalalaka had brought water in a leaf. They sat around her and talked in soft syllables, and peered at her now and then, and laughed, and evidently enjoyed her greatly. Gay smiled back. Nice people – even if the hunter was a flirt. The nicer for that, perhaps. If she were a man, though, she would flirt with Liu from dawn till dusk – and do more than flirt! ... She stopped eating, looking down the culvert.

Lady Jane Easterling and Houghton were no longer tied to the pillar. Outside, beyond the deserted doorway, came the far cry of voices.

Rather sick, Gay got to her feet. Liu got up, gesticulating that her guest was surely still hungry? Gay, with a wry smile, put her aside. What was happening out there to those two? Torture?

A remembrance of nameless bestialities, read, and shuddered upon, passed through her mind. She stumbled down the culvert and out of it, the other two at her heels.

Far below, in the oversplash from the stream, a shallow lagoon had formed in a corner of the Dam. It was to this that the entire horde of the Folk had betaken themselves. Men were swimming and mudlarking with the women. Some women were running in and out of the water with the naked children poised on their shoulders. The children screamed as they slipped off. Gay's eyes were drawn to yet another scene.

This was a group of men directly below the culvert mouth. They seemed engaged in hurling objects into the water, retrieving them, and hurling them in with an unabating enthusiasm. White objects. Gay sat down and laughed and laughed till she wept. Liu and Allalalaka laughed with her. Then the three of them went down to watch.

By then, however, the ceremony was over. Exhausted, spluttering and panting, Houghton and Lady Jane Easterling, minus their grass kilts, lay on the edge of the lagoon surrounded by their grinning jailers. Gay saw Rem and pushed a way through the throng to his side.

'That was fun. But — what else are you going to do to them?'

His grave smile came twinkling in eyes and lips at sight of her. He put out his finger to stroke her arm, and that Gay endured. She was accustomed to such things now. She rather liked them —the cat in her, she supposed. She repeated her question, standing in the centre of the group. Gasping like stranded fish, Houghton and Lady Jane listened from the ground.

Rem shook his head. 'There is nothing more. They are better now. They were mad.'

Gay nodded, solemnly. 'They were mad. Is this how you always treat the mad?'

'Unless they kill and kill. Then we kill them.'

An elementary and obvious justice. Gay said, 'Can they get up now?'

76

Rem nodded. Gay looked down at her fellow-travellers out of the twentieth century.

'They've finished with you. Got off lightly, I think.'

Lady Jane was in hysterics — angry hysterics — and Houghton, sitting up, began to comfort her. For reply he received a stinging slap in the face. The hunters grinned. Rem grinned. It was an enormous joke. The shout of mirth went echoing down the great deserted Dam.

'Idiots!'

But, saying it, she was aware of something breaking within her. Allalalaka, Liu, and Rem stared their wonder. She was suddenly, angrily, and inexplicably weeping.

iii

The Old Singer of the Folk was very old. He had seen eighty south hunting seasons, he told Gay as she squatted by his side in the blue shadows cast by the towering metallic walls on the floors of the great Dam. Presumably that was eighty years. But now he had grown so feeble and blind that the hunters had to carry him south this time, out of the rugged north, past the Echoing Pits, to this immemorial Place of yearly pilgrimage. . . .

Gay lay full length on the ground, her small breasts on the ground, her chin cupped in her hands, and listened. The great Dam drowsed. Some of the hunters had long vanished into the morning haze. Some of the children still cried and played about the shore of the lagoon, but their voices were muted in distance. The women had climbed out of the Dam, berry-hunting. Rem had disappeared. Lady Jane and Houghton were nowhere in view — probably they were inside the culvert, seeking sleep and solace for their wounded pride. Silly asses. Nice to have found the Old Man — Allalalaka had done that for her, bringing her to where he sat dreaming in the shade, and speaking a few unintelligible words to the ancient — a little shrunken man, lifting sightless eyes to Gay's face. Then he had spoken English:

'You are the woman of whom Rem told me?'

Gay had said gently: 'I think so. I know Rem.'

He had nodded and patted the ground beside him. Gay had squatted down. Relieved, the flirtatious hunter had sat silent and remote a long time after that. Then:

'Where do you come from that you speak English? What is your Folk?'

Gay had chewed at the leaf of a dock, growing on a driftage of earth gathered on the great metal floor. 'I don't think I should tell you that. You wouldn't believe me.'

The thin ancient had looked puzzled. 'Not believe?'

'You would think I did not speak the truth.'

'But I am also a Singer — as Rem is. Therefore I would know your Song.'

Gay had tried to work this out. 'Then only Singers don't speak the truth?'

'Surely. They set tales upon the truth, to make it more true.'

'Sounds sophistry to me. Don't others ever fail to speak the truth?'

He shook his head. 'Why should they?'

Why indeed? Gay looked around her, stretching her arms and toes. A strange gladness came over her. It was not only her clothes she had shed! . . . She said, 'Then perhaps I am a Singer, and also have a Song to tell. But I would like to hear yours first — not a Song, but the truth. First, is there any other Folk than this?'

He nodded. He was very old and full of memories, told in that sing-song English of perhaps two hundred words vocabulary . . . Folk? There was the Folk of the North — perhaps equal in number to themselves, the Folk of the Place. The Northern Folk sometimes came down as far as the hunting grounds of the Place Folk. But they preferred their own hunts — far away, among the great beasts. They hunted these beasts with long spears, and in the Dark Days, because of the cold, wrapped themselves in the skins of beasts.

'And do the Northern Folk and your Folk never fight?'

'Once I fought a Northern man. It was for a woman. And when we had finished fighting she said she would have neither of us. So we were sad, and went away on a lone hunt, and missed the season, and wandered through dark countries for three seasons. But that was long ago.'

'But does your Folk never go to war with the Northern Folk?'

'War? . . . That is only in the madness from the Voices.'

Gay raised her head to look away up over the frowning bastions of the Dam at the Tower raising its four hundred feet of airy metallic structure into the noon heat a quarter of a mile away. She resolved she would have that place investigated very shortly . . . . The Old Singer was reminiscent:

'He was Gara, the Northern hunter with whom I wandered. He was killed by a panther beside the Great Western Water. We came on that Water in a time of frost and mist, and it was painted with pictures. It was as we stood and watched the pictures that the panther leapt on Gara.'

Some unimaginable Scotchman. . . . 'What were the pictures?'

'It was of another country, but like our own, that hung in the sky.'

Ireland. Probably that had been Ireland. Suddenly Gay's inward vision lifted. Not England only — Ireland — America, China, the great wastes of India and Africa — this fall and passing of civilisation must have come on them all. But was that certain — might this not be a single land abandoned while civilisation went elsewhere? She asked the Old Singer if he had ever been to the Great Water in the South?

He shook his head. 'But once a woman I knew went there — she and her lover — and they came to a high cliff and saw a land remote across the Water. There were great beasts in the waters also. They went there because of the old Song of the Last Man who came from that country.'

Gay asked when that had been, and heard a dim story of a story handed down through countless generations — of a man who had crossed that water on the drifting branches of a tree, and landed, and survived, and strayed up here to the Place, and had been adopted by the Folk. He had been as themselves, but of different speech.

France. A lost Frenchman. Years and years ago, an accidental driftage of the winds and tides. Gay thought of the busy shipping that had once crowded the Channel, of the

79

hum and roar of the aeroplane in which she herself had crossed to Paris for a weekend. And now it was only a dream —a song long past.

The sunset of humankind. . . .

She looked up at the wizened ancient, brown and tough and naked, with his thin, gnarled hands and perfect teeth, lithe and compact, a Singer and hunter nearing even death: and for some reason remembered the last old man she had seen in London. It had been outside Paddington Station, and he had been selling match-boxes on the kerb —a battered old man with a face like a decaying fungus, green and horrible, his rags foul and slovenly as though they also were decaying, his eyes — they had made her almost sick, his eyes, the hopeless fear and death in them. That was what it had meant for the masses of the people since they built the first Pyramid — toil and taboos and slimy food and a slimy death. And now, in the sunset of mankind, this wind and sun and this old hunter!

'And now,' he was saying, 'you will tell me your song?'

iv

So she told it, trying to tell in simple words of that world out of which she had come and the means through which she had come. She told of the compact with Houghton and Lady Jane and their awakening on the mounds of Pewsey a week before; she told of their terror and dismay at finding themselves in the strange country in which they had come. . . . The Old Singer of the Folk sat and listened and nodded his head. He was very old. There seemed an odd note in the queer sing-song of his Voice-learned English as she finished.

'And before this coming to our Times — how did your Folk live?'

So Gay tried to tell him of that as well, to picture the great cities with their crowdings of traffic, the wheeling lights of Broadway and Piccadilly, the long roads that scarred the countryside, the massed chimneys of factories, unemployed men in long queues awaiting tokens for the purchase of food, the thunder and clang of the railway stations, the bright wheeling of aeroplanes against sunset skies. She fell in a dream and a vision herself as she talked, seeing and remembering so much of her life: she told of the march of the sciences, and how disease and death were fought; the great works of the great Singers, the great men who taught the kindlier religions. And then she found herself telling him of the Wars. . . .

When she had finished she thought for a long time that the ancient was asleep. Then he opened his sightless eyes:

'That was a Song.'

For a little she did not understand, then he said again, with peculiar stress, 'That was a Song.'

'It's the truth,' Gay said.

'It is a Song — but an evil Song. Like those that the Voices once told in the Place here. But now they are stilling one by one — every hunting season one or the other is stilling. Soon all of them will be dead, and the Folk come no more to this Place. Rem and I are the last of the Folk to learn the tongue of the Voices. When we pass, that also will pass. And the Folk do not hear the Song you sing, Gay Hunter.'

'You mean I mustn't tell them of where I came from, how I came here?'

'It is a mad Song. Rem may hear it; he also will know it mad — a thing that belongs to the past ages of our Folk. Now there are other Songs.'

Gay lay and thought, with her head in her hands. There had been the ghost of a threat in the ancient's voice. And suddenly, though he said nothing more, she realised why. He knew that her story was no mere 'song'. He knew it the truth — dimly — and he would hold her from telling it. Perhaps in his youth there had been Singers who also knew the truth of such things as she told — passed down through generations of bards and story-tellers. And now it was fading from the minds of men — allowed to fade, gladly to fade. She said:

'I am not the only one who has come. There are two others.'

'The Folk know that they have been mad, for they killed. So they will not heed them.'

Gay said, with sudden resolution, 'I cannot promise — not until I have heard those damned Voices.'

The still figure hardly moved, though the grey head nodded. 'Rem will take you to hear them at sunset.'

Far into the west the sunset was dying in a shroud, a fleece of flame. Below cowered the westering forest, and the colour dipped and played like birds through the thick-leaved boughs. All the air was very still as Gay and the hunter climbed up the winding paths worn by the feet of millennia from the floor of the Dam. Gay breathed deeply and looked down, and saw the evening parties of hunters winding back across the deserted Floor. They looked like ant-men in that great depth.

Then, the sunset in her eyes, she turned and looked again at the Tower; and, as she looked, heard in the stillness the *lap-lap-lap* of a lapwing's flight.

Now she saw that it rose, immense and airy, from a great metallic substructure besieged by bush and flowering scrub. Through this wilderness led the vestige of a path, but one long untrodden, for thorns reached their tendrils across it and the grass grew lank and high. It was a desolate, dim place, and very silent.

She glanced at Rem, leading the way. A kind of solemnity, though no fear, had fallen across his dreaming remoteness. She thought, 'Anyhow, you *have* nice flanks,' and found that homely fact comforting in this eerie place.

So it was they came to steps, and from these to a great empty doorway. Once, above the architrave, there had been inscribed some saying of the antique men. But it had been set on the metal in some kind of enamel, and only here and there did the winding scrolls persist, enigmatic, untranslatable. What had they said, what told? What had been the purpose of this Tower above the great ruined Dam?

Now she found herself within the threshold. Here the dust — metallic dust — lay inches thick. Somewhere high in the structure a beam of the departing sunlight rayed down from the roof, and she saw all the place dimly in its radiance that reflected away, faintly and ever more faintly, into the corridors of metal, into the dull-gleaming masses of apparatus that stood in silence and disuse on either side of the doorway. She had never known much of mechanical contrivances — and a ghost of regret stirred in her because of that fact, and then passed. How it would have helped her, in this maze of wheels and long, gleaming rods and time-untouched pointers and dials!

Then she saw that some indeed of the great machines were not time-untouched. One had had a cup — of glass or some such sand-product — and it had broken and spilled from itself some material that left a wide stain on the metal containers. There were other structures that fell away lopsidedly, leaning on their neighbours, with bars and keyboards grotesquely askew. These, she guessed, had had subsidiary parts made not of the yellow-brown metal, but of more perishable substances — wood or steel or glass — known to her time.... She lowered her eyes from the bewildering array to Rem, who had halted beside her. He was looking across the great dusty floor at a machine that rose like a giant organ remote in the dimness.

Towards it Gay now saw that a track had been worn in dust — towards it and none of the other machines. Yet the silting and moving of the dust, in the winds that played from the doorway and ventilation hole, had sprayed a thick covering over even that track. Gay asked a question, and, asking it, gave a little cry and gasped at Rem's arm. For the question was caught and spun and re-echoed savagely about the building, till it seemed to Gay it must be shouted abroad all the sunset countryside:

'When did you last come here?'

'The Old Singer brought me here three hunting seasons ago.'

Three years before.... Gay looked into the dimness and then again at Rem. He nodded and they crossed the dusty track together. Crossing, their coming, soundless though it was, stirred great clouds of bats in those remote darknesses. The air grew alive with the fuff-fuff of their wings. And now, within touch of the great organ-like machine, Gay saw that all around the floor and the walls were thick with the droppings of bats. Then she saw a grislier sight. Over to the right lay a skeleton. An outstretched, bony hand reached up to a thing like a typewriter keyboard. A key had been wrenched down and remained down.... It had all happened years before.

Rem paid it no heed. He had halted in front of the

thing like a great organ. But it was no organ, though Gay never saw its shape plainly, though her mind retained a blurred impression of voluting spirals and great pipe-like structures reaching up into invisibility. At the height of a man from the floor two little levers — they could not have been more than a foot in length — projected from the machine through narrow, dusty slots. Rem was looking at those; then he turned his shadowed, amber eyes.

'This is where the Voices speak. There are many voices — beginning many tales, some in words that we do not know. Once they thundered, the Old Singer has told me, but now they are sometimes no more than a whisper. You must pull this stick.'

He pointed to the right-hand lever, and then squatted in the dust. Gay stood and stared at the dim machine.

What would happen? What was she to hear? Any whisper at all of her own times and the innumerable voices that had cried through them of the things that would come to the world? What profit, indeed, to hear those Voices when all of which they told and hoped was no more now than dust a-blow in a ruined Tower, a whisper at night as the dark came down?

So she stood a long time in hesitation, the strayed young American girl in the Chilterns Tower; then she put up her hand to the lever Rem had indicated, and pulled it down — it came with a little click — and herself sank down in the dust by the side of Rem.

At that moment the beam of sunlight suddenly vanished, and far off, through the open door, Gay saw the day dying from the land.

8. The Hierarchs

i

IT MUST have been towards three o'clock in the morning when Gay, lost far away in the depths of the forest beyond the Dam, raised her head from her arms. A breath of night wind sighed in the trees, but as she looked up she saw the stars paling, and low in the east a smoulder where the moon had gone down. She covered her face with a moan, and sank down on the unseen grass again, remembering the horror of that Voice that had whispered and whispered in the ruined Tower as the moon rose over the Chilterns.

Great patches had faded from her mind (protective instinct had seen to that), leaving only a track of remembrance like the slime of a snake's passing; but others remained searing in her mind as with red-hot coals. . . . She covered her ears to shut herself away from the encompassing silence.

'It was a lie that the Voice told — horrible lies!'

That cool, cynical Voice — had it been capable of lying? — It, with its tale of the culmination of the world's civilisations and their last downfall in war and riot? It had been the weary Voice of civilisation itself, whispering from the dust, dust only, without any rosy guisings of flesh that had guised the foul thing it outlasted. . . . She remembered now, she and Rem squatting in the dust, the whirr and whisper as some needle apparatus had engaged on some unimaginable record. At first the Voice had been in no language that she knew —though that meant little. She knew only a few of the European languages. It might have been Russian, Chinese, Esperanto, Volapuk. It had gone on for a long time, a whisper, but a genuine re-echoing, she had understood even then, of a human voice that had once breathed on the apparatus of the strange machine. Thousands of years before. . . .

The Tower had grown ever darker as they listened;

and in a little she had been unable to see even the brown face and figure of the Singer, Rem, beside her. And then, abruptly:

'I have been commissioned by the [indistinguishable] to make these records for the broasting station by the Chiltern Dam. They are made in some haste and confusion, for it is now only a matter of a day or so (we think) before the attack of the Transatlantics. Already most of the European Great Centres have been obliterated by atomic bombs, and only the fact that the Fascist Federation has sent its fleet to delay the Transatlantics still saves London. But we do not imagine that our immunity will last long. The Army of the Communes is on the march from the north, and everywhere the sub-men have risen, destroying the ways and killing and devouring the overseers. So the Great Council has made direction for the making of this record and others to place in the unburnable station protected by its water-belts. It seems that the end has now come in the north as already in Australasia and Africa, and the War Plagues are following the outbreak. . . . Our chemists are still attempting, and so far unsuccessfully, to cope with the poisoning dust that comes from the atomic bombing. . . .'

The Voice had died away then, a little silence had followed, and then another Voice had taken its place, this time in a strange, twisted German — a German fined of its nouns and with a slimmer and easier verb than Gay remembered. It did no more than repeat the substance of the first record in English; then again came that English Voice. It plunged into a rapid survey of the rise of the Great Hierarchies.

They had risen, it seemed, several hundred years before that time in which the Voice spoke, at a time when humanity had been at the cross-roads. . . . There were innumerable interpolations here, and a point where the whisper had failed entirely. Then it resumed, history-telling, with a cold brevity.

'So the great order of the War States arose, and the sub-men were allotted to those classes from which the Hierarchs drew their helots and servants. The great problem of surpluses was solved, and everywhere the Hierarchies entered into control of those States that have made our civilisation; so that in comparison with them the greatest achievements of the earliest scientific age of the old

86

Christ-age superstition are little more than the fumblings of savages in the dark. We have measured the stars and sent ships to the planets, we have prolonged life and mitigated death, created new life in the test-tubes of our laboratories, altered the periodicity of the seasons, reached in the arts the verge of a world that definitely marks a new and subtle transformation of the human mind. But now it seems that all this glorious fabric may be either completely or partially levelled in the Revolt of the Sub-Men . . . '

The moon had come up and Gay had raised a blind look to it as the Voice whispered on and on – of those Sub-Men, their world-wide revolt, the condition of their lives, how they were mated and bred in pens, and looked to with a scientific care… Once Gay had crept away into a corner of the dark building to be ill, and had thought of running from the Tower. But the Voice pursued her, whispering and whispering, and again she had trodden back through the dust to listen. Rem had sat like a statue carved in darkness – she stumbled against him and his hand had caught hers and guided her to the ground again.

Now the whispering Voice was in a blur of technicalities of which she could make nothing – it was whispering at a gabble innumerable formulae and recipes it believed of supreme importance for members of the Hierarchies to know should they survive the debacle. Gay caught a glimpse of great machines and skyey towers and the roar of aircraft in an alien sky, the mixing of metals and the making of books; then all drifted away in a sudden jar of the machine; and again an alien language took up the tale.

So through long hours it had seemed to go on, she sitting it seemed in a giant auditorium, watching the play of the last centuries of civilisation: how men had grown as no beasts that had ever lived – splendid, immense, terrible and cruel: while underneath festered the Sub-Men, the Ancient Lowly. That Voice whispered of the Hierarchies' triumphs, their tremendous wars, their passions and pleasures.... Once Gay fainted while it told of their pleasures. Then it told of the suppressing of a former revolt of the Sub-Men – an international revolt – how thousands of the Sub-Men had been crucified up and down the stretches of the Atlantic coasts. Now war had broken out, to an extent never suffered before, between the Hierarchies, and everywhere the Sub-Men had risen in a last tremendous revolt.... And these were the last records, the last records; but before the Hierarchs perished this was their Testament of Life, these the things by which they lived....

It was, Gay remembered now, at the whisper of the second code in that Testament that she had found the listening unendurable. Something had seemed to crack in her brain as she listened to the filth that the Voice whispered. She had jumped to her feet and fled — fled from the Tower out into the moonlighted world beyond, with the trees waving dark against the dim horizon. To those trees she had turned with racing, heedless steps — anywhere, anyhow, out of hearing of that abomination in the Tower. The trees — the trees — God, for the shelter and danger of the trees!

Once, far behind her as she fled and ran and stumbled down alleyways of the forest, she thought she heard someone cry. But that crying faded and presently died from her hearing.

ii

So it was as the dawn came that Gay got to her feet and fled north again, through the hill and jungle of that England lost far in time. She had no plan or route in mind — for hours it was no more than a blind scurry through a shadowed day — away from the sight or sound of human kind.

Kneeling that afternoon by a stagnant pool, she looked at her reflected self — that self that had sometimes so pleased her — and shuddered with a cold disgust. What a foul thing and unclean was the human body, fit house for the sickening cruelty and shame of the human mind....

'Filth — I shall never forget it, however long I live, wherever I live. Why should I go on living at all — sick as I am with it? God, so sick! Beasts — there were never beasts like the human beasts that have been....'

She remembered then the great heroes of the human march in the far-off times before her own century — Akhnaton and the Christ, Spartacus, the Buddha: those who

88

had believed in the triumph of the kindly and the free, those whom men had taken as beacon lights for two long millennia. And their dreams had sunk into pits of slime, devoured and befouled in a more cruel aberration of the human spirit than the blood-sacrificing Aztecs ever knew. For *that* all the ages had visioned and hoped — for that horror whispered by the Voice in the Tower.

'But it's finished and ended — that civilisation that became a nightmare. Now, at least there are no crucified helots lining the Atlantic shores; even the names of those people are no more than dying whispers.... I suppose after all there was a God. And He endured men till they sickened Him, and then wiped out that crazy building of toys like a nurse a cruel child's toy-prison. Ended and finished.'

Where would she go, where could she hide, in what place in the hills where never again she would be sickened by the sight of a human face? Somewhere — some place she would get to — till the winter came and killed her.

And, with that resolve, a strange new freshness came on Gay's tired body.

She would go west.

iii

That night she was awakened by the crackle of a broken twig below a hesitating footstep.

She raised her head. It was Rem; behind him in the moonlight glimmered the eyes of his wolf.

9. Persephone

i

HE SAID: 'I followed you from the Tower.'

That, she thought, too plain to need comment. Then an involuntary shiver of disgust came on her, looking up at the naked figure standing in the moonlight. She had thought she had escaped them all — and here was this fool, this brainless savage with his nakedness and his bow and his dog and his eyes of a moron — following her even here. She said:

'Go away. Go back. I don't want you.'

He stood still for a second, then turned about, the wolf at his heels, and disappeared into the leafy corridors of the forest.

She had not thought she would be taken at her word — so immediately. Something stung in her throat and she swallowed and blinked back the tears. Then rage came in place of dismay. The fool — the degenerate clown! She wanted nothing to do with him —never wanted to see him again! He and all the crowd of the Folk who sheltered in the culverts above the Chiltern Dam — what were they but degenerate survivors of that catastrophe that had smitten the last civilisation of the filthy human race? Degenerates, slow-witted and beastly and cool because they were brainless. And that fool Rem — she blinked angry tears — the worst of the lot.

An owl screamed close at hand. A little shiver of fear seized her. What if there were panthers in this forest — or bears? Hadn't she best climb a tree?

Odd how the will to live went on! She, who had looked on suicide only a day back with passion and purpose, was now afraid of a very obvious and plain and useful death! Killed and eaten by a beast, she would serve at least some useful purpose. This disgusting fear of the disposal of one's body....

90

She lay and thought, in the moonlighted forest, of all those fearful dreams that had smitten men on death and the hope of survival beyond death — the cavemen of France and Spain who buried their kind wrapped in red earth, the colour of blood, that blood might revivify them to new hunting-grounds; the clownish kings of the early Nile and their gigantic sepulchres, the pyramids; Zoroastrian exposure; Keltic fire-burning — a scum and a leprosy on the mind of men, that fear and care for death. What part had she with it — she, who had renounced her kind and all their filthy preoccupations?

'Damn you,' she whispered to the waiting forest, 'come and kill me, then!'

Far off, in the depths of the trees, a jungle-cock crowed drowsily in its sleep.

ii

In the week that followed, in the same daze of indifference, she lived such life as in memory was to leave her breathtaken with amazement.

She wandered on, west and north-west, indifferent to her surroundings, through land of hill and rolling grassland and recurrent forest. She came once to a blackened tundra where a great fire had been, and set out to cross it, indifferent to the fact that she might die of hunger. And she did not die, for midway was an unburned copse — a copse of apple trees, and a clear spring of water. So, perforce, she fed, and went on again, after an indifferent glance at herself in the water of the spring. So glancing, she had seen a soiled, sooty gnome, like one of those horrific pictures of the mourning women of the ancient Indonesian Islands.

In a path in the bush she came on a great bear. The beast snuffled at her and growled warningly, half-rising on his hind legs. She heard herself laugh, and did not moderate her pace, her eyes bitter and blind as she went towards that awaiting death. Then the bear, sniffing the air in the direction from which she came, shambled away, grumblingly, into the bush. She passed on.

She climbed a great tree one night to a leafy bower and lay there under the dew and the stars. It was the night of a great fall of shooting stars — the Leonids, she thought, and lay awake, pricked to a faint interest in the celestial performance. Then she laughed drearily — what were stars to her, what had men ever seen in them but their own fancies? And she had ceased to play with the cloacal fancyings of men.

Sometimes she heard herself singing, singing like a lost soul in Hades, a dim Hades of a pagan faith. Then she would wander on in a numb silence. Now she was in country alive with game. Long, one evening, on the verge of a great treey park, she stood and watched wild cattle at graze, great herds of them with their bulls and calves, dun beasts, with here and there speckled, shaggy monsters that might have been descendants of the Highland cattle of antiquity. It was an unhunted land. The beasts hardly raised their heads as she set out to cross the park through their midst.

Next day she recognised the country through which she travelled. It was the Vale of the White Horse. South, crowned with rain-clouds, rose again the Downs. Now the weather had changed from its undeviating sunshine, and long streamers of mist covered the land each morning. Now she went slower, for a certain weakness had come on her with the lack of food, the indifferent food she ate. She was aware of various disgusting bodily inconveniences. A wild taggle-haired creature looked at her from this pool and that, with staring eyes and a strained, starved face, and she looked back now at the reflection with a vague interest, lying long whiles (they seemed long hours), to stare down at the mirrored self that had once given her delight. Before . . . .

She got to her feet and staggered on again. Late in the afternoon of the sixth day she found a fault in the chalk hills and crept in there. Some seismic disturbance had gutted the rock of a great handful of chalk, leaving a place rocky and inhospitable enough inside, but yet a place where she could die. A little river wound out of the chalk below. She drank there, and then groped her way into the cave with the last of the light.

From long, tormented dreams in the days and nights that followed she came back slowly to the outside world, to life again, to hearing that sweet, unending shrill of the stream, night and day, the hours of sun and the hours of shadow, the hours when Rem sat at the cave-mouth and sharpened an arrow, his face dappled in the fall of shadows from the beech tree near; the hours when the dark came down and she heard him breathing beside her, the wolf Towser lying across the cave-mouth; the hours when the cave was pelted with rain, and she looked out on a steaming landscape. . . . Deep and haunting the rill of the stream went on.

Only slowly, disentangling dream from fact, had the consciousness come on her that Rem and the wolf had followed her and found her — dying, she supposed, a strayed Persephone in the Hades of her own imaginings. She had been conscious of hands below her and about her, of herself being moved, of a time — it must have been night — when the hunter was kindling a fire against the cold. She had lain and watched him with wondering eyes, and then slipped away into sleep. Sleep — she seemed to sleep and sleep as though to make up for the wakefulness of ten millennia!

But at last, one morning, she was strong enough to sit up, in the nest of grass the hunter had made her, and ate earth-baked rabbit and half-raw eggs — milk or soup was beyond the hunter's reach. (Milk, indeed, that most unnatural of foods, was unknown to the Folk.) She found herself with a ravenous appetite and the sun shining on an early morning landscape; and Rem, amber-eyed, squatting a little distance away.

'How did you find me?'

'I followed you.'

'My tracks — the marks I had left?'

'I was always with you — a little distance behind you.'

She sat and wondered about that, her hunger a little appeased. 'Then — then that was why the bear — oh, days ago —slunk off into the bushes. . . . And I thought it was my own ferocity scared it! And that was why . . . '

Lying back again, she thought of a multitude of whys.

But she would not bother much about them, now. Goodness, how good it was to be alive, even though she felt dirt-engrained from head to foot and the cave was smelly with human habitation! She sat up again, slowly.

'I don't think I can walk yet. Will you help me over to the door of the cave?'

For a moment he did not understand. Then he came and bent down and picked her up. He picked her up as easily as though she were a child. She said:

'That was neat. Just down on our doorstep, please.'

Still he waited, holding her, not moving. She raised her head, reluctantly, slowly, and looked up into his face.

Clown? Savage? Degenerate? Moron? ... With a catch of breath she realised she had never looked deeply in those amber eyes before, into deep golden pools where shadows and strange images moved and changed and took fresh being — endlessly, unceasingly, not as the thought-images of the men she had known, confused and mixed and broken, but with the assurance and sweep of clouds in the sky. And out of them one thought shone and abided a moment, so that she looked at it, strangely, yet not afraid, with a kind of quick wonder. She said, again, though this time in a whisper:

'I think you'd better put me down.'

He carried her then to the mouth of the cave, and propped her there, and she closed her eyes to the sun-dazzle. Then he came back and packed grass about her and under her, and still with eyes closed she let him do that. She heard him moving about the cave, and looked up and saw him with his bow and two arrows in his hand.

'Hunting?'

He nodded. For a moment they smiled at each other, and again that odd breathlessness took Gay. Then he was walking away from the cave. The wolf Towser got to his feet, but Rem gestured him back towards the cave. Gay realised the reason — he was to protect her.

Yawning, the wolf came back and lay flat in the sunlight, bright eyes on Gay. She put out a brown hand on his head, still staring after the hunter. Rem. The Singer.

'Goodness, Towser, and I thought I hated all men! ... But I suppose I'd forgotten so much I learned — centuries ago.

Rem the real man: not those poor ghosts who lived long ago and still whisper in the Tower. Rem . . . '

He would not bear thinking about, too intimately. She closed her eyes and began to move legs and arms and fingers and toes. They had been cramped and stiff, but now she could feel the run and trill of blood awakening within them — magic and strange, as if in rhythm with the trill and quiver of the water in the hidden stream beyond the cave. Beyond that stream the great valley rose and quivered, southwards, up to the lone heights of the Wiltshire Downs. Somewhere, as on that first morning at Pewsey, curlews were crying.

'The Woman Who Came Back. After Many Years. . . . I could stand as the moral of a dozen novelettes. Many Waters Cannot Quench. . . . '

She stopped that amused whisper and ruffled Towser's head. 'Somehow that last quotation's inappropriate — to laugh at, anyway. How long do you think he'll be, Towser?'

The wolf lifted up questioning eyes, yawned, and dropped his head to his paws again. Gay nodded, drowsily.

'Sorry to be a bore. Anyhow, he'll be safe enough. Wake me when he comes.'

She was sun-tired and sleepy still when Rem himself awoke her. The sun was slanting towards afternoon. And a portion of slaughtered calf was grilling on sticks in front of the fire — the smoke wound up blue, pencilled and still from the fire. Gay looked from the meat to the hunter, and rubbed her eyes.

'I feel I could eat all that calf. . . . Do you know that in the times from which I came, Rem, there were people who were horrified that animals were killed and eaten? Horrified that they were cleanly killed and eaten, and yet took it quite as a matter of fact that their own fellow-humans starved in diseased slums. Long ago, before the days of the Voice — what *did* you do with the Voice, by the way?'

'I moved the other stick, and the Voice stopped. Then I followed you.'

'I know you did. You're a dear. Anyone ever told you that before?'

He pondered on this, and shook his shapely, bearded head. 'Deer?'

Gay said, 'Not the running kind. The static. Don't

95

let's bother. How long have I lain in the cave?'

He counted that back carefully: 'Seven days.'

Gay thought: 'So it's a fortnight since I ran away from the Tower. It feels like — but I'm beginning to disbelieve in time altogether.... No, I don't want food yet, I've decided. Oh, I'm quite well. But I want a bath instead. You couldn't make love to me unless I had a bath — could you?'

He was puzzled. 'Make — love?'

She stood and regarded him lightedly, a hand on the side of the cave in case she should grow dizzy again. He had never heard of the word? Not from her; not from the horrific record of the whispering voice. 'You don't know what "love" is?'

He shook his head, the amber eyes kindled from their remoteness, a little, nevertheless, as he looked at her. Gay said: 'Well, I'll teach you — sometime, maybe, if I ever succeed in scrubbing down to my own skin. I'm a horribly modest female; but you shouldn't have followed me and rescued me — and then looked at me like that!'

He stood and watched her run down to the stream and gather great handfuls of chalky earth by its bank and slip out of his sight. A noise of splashing came up to the cave. The fire crackled softly. He followed the bather.

iv

They played a splashing game for hours in that stream and the osiers that fringed its side. The wolf ran and frisked about them, and roused a hare, and went off in chase of it. Gay scrambled out at last to the bank, and looked down at herself, and liked herself again. She felt very tired from the unwonted exertions — hips and spine ached. Rem came to where she lay and put out his hands on her. She said, startled:

'What?' And then: 'Oh, massage? Do, lots of it. I could do with new bones!'

She felt in a few minutes that her wish had come true. Presently it had done more than that. She wriggled away from those firm, suave hands. Who would have thought a hunter would have such hands? Dangerous — at least for the moment. She addressed his solemn face:

96

'I was once afraid of you, Rem. Long ago. Remember that meeting we had among the berry-bushes? And later.... Afraid of all kind of things. Wasn't I a fool? I'm not afraid now.'

He said: 'Sometime I will teach you the speech of the Folk, and you will forget all that the Voices tell. The Voices are dying.'

She stretched her hands and then put them behind her head and leaned back on the warm grass in the lighted summer day. 'Sometime you'll teach me all that. We've years to teach each other.' She sat up. 'Goodness — but have we? You may have done all this just because I'm a freak and a curiosity — not wanting me at all.' She stared at him dismayed and shameless and earnest. 'Do you want to sleep with me?'

He did not understand the euphuism. She thought of another word that the Voice had used in place of that shameful snigger of the twentieth century and, using it, saw herself, globed and earnest, in the hunter's eyes. Then her image vanished, and in its place came hurrying a multitude of lighted torches.... She moved away a little.

'So you do.' She was shamelessly relieved. 'And for always?'

'Always — while I shall want to.'

She paused, in doubt of that; and then nodded. 'Reasonable and sane.... No, but not yet. My dear, can't you allow a strayed female out of the abysses to remember just a little of the slushy romance that once guarded such lives as hers? Your whole life is a song: ours — the flopping dirges they were!'

The wolf came back through the bushes and laid a hare at Rem's feet, and looked up into his face with such earnestness it was obvious that he at least had missed his dinner. So Rem and Gay stood up, Gay white still beside the brown hunter, and returned to the cave to bestir the fire. With the so doing a fury of housekeeping energy came on Gay. She gathered a handful of twigs and swept out the cave and its litter, and brought in grass for two new grass beds, and ... She looked about her. There was nothing else for her to do.

Strange place for a bridal chamber — a cave in the hills wihout even a bed, a wardrobe, or a dressing-mirror. No place of tradition or antique custom to hide one from the other; furnishings, goods or possessions to worry over or have pride in. (But sometimes that fact faded from your mind, so sane and earnest was this existence, and you had to say it over to yourself again and again — stark! Starker than ever the souls in the Christian God's day of judgment!) Instead ...

She thought of the brides throughout the thousands of years of civilisation — the willing and unwilling, the child-brides of India, the obscene rites of betrothal and marriage, veiling and unveiling, the dirty jests and the lewd comments. She thought of fantastic rites of sacrifice, of brides who gave the first night to a priest or a stranger, of the seigneur's right in ancient France, of all the strange, unclean garmentings that had swathed the delight and beauty — oh, and she supposed, agony, of something clean and natural and terrible as sun and wind. ... So she supposed it was, she had never known.

She looked at Rem, recumbent, cooking, long-legged and naked and brown, his muscles rippling like long snakes as he moved, his head wet and glossy with the splashings in the stream. For a second something cold held her heart, so alien and strange he looked. And then that vision of him with twentieth-century eyes quite went from her, never to return again.

Abruptly, far south on the scarred edges of the Downs, lightning flashed a long jagged tooth. Gay started, with a leg of hare in her hand — almost jugged hare in the start. Shame if it came rain now after a day like this.

Come it did, however, the clouds piling all the southern sky in black cumulus through which the lightning played. Then it swept up north in driving sheets, the rain, and the three of them drew back in the cave and watched its coming, hissing. Gay looked round for utensils and goods to retrieve from outside. There were none. She sat down and clasped her knees, on the edge of the cave and the spit of the rain, and watched the wet closing in of the evening.

The long silences of such evenings — silences which once men had had to seek as they sought gold and glittering stones! Silence in which nothing cried but the lapwings, no sound to be heard but the brill of a stream going home to the sea, and far and away, in the east, the belling of some stray bull of a Titan herd. ... It had grown dark, quite suddenly, the night coming down with the rain in a little hiss that fell on the fire the hunter had brought half-way within the cave-shelter. How blessed was his silence as well — one could roll oneself in the cloak of it and dream for ever, as he did himself. But this evening. . . .

She put out a hand and it clasped round his foot in the fire-sprayed dimness. A very young foot, athletic and hard, but the skin of it as young as her own.

'You're the Singer, Rem, and you sing only for the Folk. But isn't there anything you can sing for ourselves — just this once?'

A hand came down into the light of the fire and settled firmly on the hand on his foot. And then, without warning, crouched where he was, he began to sing.

It was in alien words of which she knew nothing. She knew little indeed of any kind of singing, and she thought that once (in her half-forgotten world) that voice of his would have been an untrained contralto, strangely girlish emerging from that rounded and vigorous throat. But it rose into an easy ecstasy of which she had never heard the like — as though his whole being sang, not lips and palate and chest only, but every fibre of his body, till the cave was filled with the melody of the sound and, like a gigantic trumpet, flung the sound out into the raining night in a triumphant pæan. Higher and deeper and richer it rose; and now, though she knew as little as ever of the words, the meaning seemed clear to Gay, in great stretches and flashes of vision and recognition. . . . She saw the play and wash and laughter of water in the sun, she heard the crying of hunters in the hunt, smelt the smoke of the great forests on fire, heard the beat and drum of blood in a body that raced the sunrise in the spring when the first beech-buds put out. All these, and the heat and din and drum of summer he sang, the voice of the rain and the voice of the stars, innumerable the voices of the stars, his song grown austere and white and terrible. And the melody dropped and changed and the day came again and the day was the bridal day of the earth — clouds on the earth with their sweeping rains that laid seed for fruit and flower, the mating cattle in their great pastures, the mating of birds in the deeps of the woods, the mating of all living things that turned in strained

99

delight to the supremest ecstasy. He sang the rivers and the hills and the sky, and all life brought to passion and the bridal bed and the loveliness of love.....

Gay could find no words when he had finished – could do nothing but still clasp that foot in a kind of frightened exaltation. Then he said, breathing deeply (she could feel the clean sweat pringling on his body because of that passion of singing that had been his):

'Sing for me.'

'I? Oh, what could I sing but wasn't futile and foolish in comparison with that? Singer, we had no Songs — except sometimes old things, peasant things, before they broke the minds and hearts of your ancestors in the mills of civilisation. Little scraps and fragments, and they grow dim for me already.'

'Sing one for me.'

Then she remembered and sang for him a German song of her mother's, a song of the low Elbe and the mists and ripening sun there; and *Criébe,* that was sung in Provence. And last of all, a verse of Swinburne's that her father had set to music and had once declared was the loveliest thing ever written by that tormented, castrated poseur:

> *'I hid my heart in a nest of roses,*
> *Out of the sun's way, hidden apart;*
> *In a softer bed than the soft white snow's is,*
> *Under the roses I hid my heart,*
> *Why would it sleep not? Why should it start,*
> *When never a leaf of the rose-tree stirred?*
> *What made sleep flutter his wings and part?*
> *Only the song of a secret bird.'*

When the echoes of her own singing had died away, Gay felt the hunter's hands on her, firmly, gently, shaking her from that world of dreams. She rose and stretched and looked down at the fire, heaped with rotten branches and half-sodden bushes. It burned with a low and a clean smell, into the wastes of the raining night. She stretched her arms and turned for another look at that night.

No stars, no moon; but she heard, shrill and unbroken, the voice of the stream. She turned from it, glad.

'And now I suppose it's the great moment. And even now I must joke about it to hide its face. Soon be love, Rem, and I — I have never known it before... But, O Singer of Persephone, if you knew the relief it is that you can't say, "I love you!"'

10. The Moon in Ajalon

i

IN THE days that followed it seemed to Gay that the world stood still to listen to that song of a secret bird in her heart. It was not only the magic and wonder of the fulfilment of her body: it was as though she were all the starved and cheated women of all time who had mated in shame, inadequately, hemmed in by codes and taboos and shames — she was their justification, in her their dim, sad lives found harbour. She would stare at herself with secret wonder, those hours of rain and sunshine, and shut her eyes fast, and open them again — surely she had dreamt it all! ... And there would be Rem and his wolf — real as the hills, and more enduring, the hills could crumble to dust — hearing that song of a secret bird as she herself heard it unendingly.

'*Sun, stand thou still over Gibeon; and thou, moon in the Valley of Ajalon.*'

They tramped and explored and flirted and fled and hid from each other for miles around the wild land that drew to a focus in their chalk-pit cave. They spent long hours in the stream and drying on the bank, half-awake, half-asleep, with the sun upon them and sometimes the rain, and delight in both. One night Rem took her back through the eastern forest fringe to the edge of the great llano. As they neared it she heard a thunderous bellowing, and in the starlight saw a sight she would never forget. The great herds of wild cattle were in migration, southwards, moved by some common impulse, mysterious and unnameable. Every late hunting season, the hunter told her, they went south like this, a bronze-black torrent. At their flanks and their heels in the dim light Gay saw the shapes of slinking carnivores — panthers and bigger beasts, greatly maned. They followed the herds and paid no heed to Gay or her hunter or the wolf that squatted growling at their feet. Gay stared after the great cats incredulously. It was impossible; but it was a fact.

They were lions.

How had such beasts ever come to England — lions or panthers? But the days were shorter and warmer than once they had been, and in the collapse of the civilisation of the Hierarchs such beasts might have broken out of zoological gardens or the like — there had been many such gardens, she had gathered from the whisper of the Voice in the Tower. Great beasts had been pets of the Hierarchs. More than pets. She shuddered with disgust at remembrance of those sickening revelations of a devilish cruelty and curiosity that had bred neo-human monsters for sport in that world which the Sub-Men rose and murdered. Oh, well that they murdered it and left it clean for the clean lust of such as Rem and herself!

Then they went back to the cave and each other's arms; and she wondered how he could make his naked, muscular shoulder so soft and seemly a pillow as always he did. And he twisted his fingers in her short black hair and played with that a long time, as he liked to do. He would sing her name in a trill that made a complete song from each syllable — it was something new in vocal power that had come into the world since her day and she would lie and listen to it with a wistful hope she might follow and comprehend. Sometime she would learn his language — sometime. She had all her life to learn it!

She would never forget the sleeping hush of those mornings when she was the first to start awake, Rem and his wolf both sound asleep and the early sun barely topping the strange beech-boughs of the eastern forest. The shine of the dew on the grass and the wakening crying of the curlews would greet her as she danced to the door of the cave and poked the fire and piled on it the brush they had gathered the previous evening. Then she would uncover the leaves from their provision for breakfast and wrinkle a hesitant nose over it, and feel germ-defyingly hungry as she scraped away the fire to bury the meat for baking. Rem and his wolf still asleep: she would bathe before they awakened.

That, and coming back glowing and dripping to find

the hunter perhaps vanished away into the scrubland of the north and returning with handfuls of cranberries, or wild plums, or great wild apples — the apples had been tamed so much by men that they had never reverted to their primal sourness or smallness.... They would sit side by side and eat, and there would be no plates or napkins or graces at all, and oh, thank Heaven, no washing-up! Then the day and its life lay all before them — to laze, to dream, to hunt, to wander without aim, in the blessedness of silence and life.

Once, straying far in the west, they came on just such a great circular space as Gay and Houghton and Lady Jane had crossed in the early days as they pressed west from Pewsey. Gay found a stick and dug here, as she had done in that far place, and, as once before, exposed the mouldering coppery surface beneath. The hunter stood and watched her inscrutably — she would never get deep in his mind after all, she thought in a moment of panic — shining and splendid though that mind was.... Then that thought went by, while she squatted, slim and dark, the mate herself of a hunter, and looked at the circular plateau from the ruined years. What purpose had it served?

Then she remembered from the whisperings of the Voice that there had been mention of 'vision plates' in the countryside, from which observers in the great hives of the Hierarchies — they had towered in great pylons miles towards heaven, those cities — had watched on the passing and acts of the Sub-Men who had served as shepherds and landserfs. This must be one of them. Her mind hesitated around the explanation, and then found it.

It was a television-plateau.

She looked up and found Rem's eyes still upon her. He shook his head.

'They are part of the Song of the Mad Men long ago. They cannot harm you now.'

'Oh, I know that. Poor, dreadful fools they were — poor beasts. But Rem — what if that madness should come on the world again? They were men very like you, those Palæolithic hunters of the Mediterranean four thousand years before Christ, on whom the first madness came — clean and kind and adorable, bright hunters, who cuddled their girls just as nicely as you cuddle yours — and painted great pictures if they didn't sing great songs. What if that madness comes back?'

He shook his head again, remote lights in the amber eyes. 'There are other Songs.'

And no more than that would he say, and Gay went on by his side and on in a long dream upon his words till his hand on her shoulder wakened her; and they crept through long grass to the edge of a natural piggery they had discovered, and lay there a long time, watching and giggling over the antics of the solemn porkers within. Crisp bacon ready to hand. . . .

Once, straying across the llanos to the south, they saw high on the crest of the Downs a crumbled metallic pylon. But it was in no such state of preservation as that Tower overtopping the great Chilterns Dam. They spent a day in the open making towards it: when night came it was still two or three miles distant, and they spent the night in the open grass-land, without fire or covering — the strangest experience of them all, all those days of crowded experience, it seemed to Gay. Night and darkness and the wind upon one, naked and unshielded and unafraid. . . . Long after Rem slept she was wakeful, lying between him and the wolf, watching the brightening of the altered stars. Then she slept and woke to the dawn red on the buttresses of the ruined pylon.

They climbed and adventured all that day amid its ruins, seeking Gay knew not what, unless it might be some intimate mark of the lives and loves and hopes of those men who had once built it and used it for a purpose long powder and nothing. But except the great metallic girders, towering to the ruined roof, and a floor thick with metallic dust, the place was empty and deserted. Wood and steel and all other furnishing it ever had had long melted away. It was obvious to Gay as they came out and looked back at the great structure that its ruin had not been through the hand of Time only: its westward side was crumpled and shattered into a pit that went deep in the earth. They wandered to the edge of that pit and she stared down at the stagnant green water.

'A shell-hole. The place was shelled.'

By whom and when? That she would never know. She turned soberly by the hunter's side and went back with him through a day's travelling to the cave that was their home. She questioned his dreaming silence and heard that he knew of still one other Tower that survived — only one, apart from that of the Voice. It was far in the north, and as ruined as the pylon of the Downs.

'But there may be others — where the Folk have never yet wandered?'

'There may be. But the Voice tells that there is only one Tower with Voices. When they have died, there will be no other Voice to sing the Ancient Madness.'

Gay had a sudden start of fear. 'But I, Gay Hunter, am not I also a Voice from the past?'

He shook his head, his arm about her, his eyes remote. 'You are the Gay Hunter.'

Something else — some warning she should tell him — vexed at the edge of its mind, but she put it away. It was so easy these days to put aside all warnings and worryings whatsoever!

That night, in the cave again, on the verge of sleep, she suddenly remembered what it was that had vexed her memory. She shook Rem's shoulder.

'There isn't only I! Remember — the other two — Houghton and Lady Jane Easterling. . . . Oh, damn it, we'd forgotten them. Rem, what if they have told tales of the Ancient Madness to the Folk?'

'But they are mad,' he said, 'and the Folk will not heed.' But there seemed a doubt in his voice.

'But once before men heeded this madness — it brought great gifts to men — ease and security and varieties in foods and cures for their hurts. What if your Folk at the Dam should heed again the madness of civilisation?'

He shook his head. 'We have other dreams.'

'What?'

But here they were at something dim and incommunicable, and Gay felt a moment, and once again, sick, alien from this dreaming Singer. What were the 'dreams'? What other thing was it that men of this time were turning to, of which she knew nothing, of which it might be she could never share? For it was not merely the hunter's environment and training that made him different from herself in a multitude of ways — so, on his arms, in his sight and hearing, she knew —

106

it was that he stood far at the thither side of a world of terror and great experience on which her own generation had barely ventured. Out of that pit they had climbed, Rem and his kind, with something vanished for ever from their minds and hearts, and something new and upgrowing in its place. They were not simply the hunters of antique time, the Cro-Magnards and the like, free of the nightmare of civilisation. They had brought from that thing, dim, no memory, but a fresh orienting of thought and will. And from its basis they were building some New Life and way of life, planning some fresh assault on the stars in a way as alien to her comprehension as the mind and mentality of the ant or the octopus.

Yet, if that was so, why need she vex at the memory of Houghton and Lady Jane Easterling, those two ludicrous strays in the Dam of the Chilterns? Why did Rem and the Old Singer wish the Voices in the Tower to die, if it came to that?

She asked him, and he stumbled amidst the English words to find an explanation:

'Because it might be that the Folk would mistake the gifts – for a little while, till they found them Bad Singing.... But it will never be.'

And then a dreadful apprehension came on Gay. 'Rem, we must go back to the Dam to-morrow. We *must*.'

'But ...'

'Do you think I want to? That I don't want this to go on for ever? But I want it to go on for others as well as ourselves.... Houghton . . . Lady Jane. Goodness, what silly little filth mayn't they have been scattering? You don't know anything about such people, my Singer. . . . Oh, they've spoilt my honeymoon for me, and I'm miserable, a savage in a cave, and lost again, and I want to cry.... Persephone up from Hades – sing for me, Rem, in case I've to go down again!'

BOOK II

GAY GO DOWN

1. The Beam

i

TOWARDS EVENING of the fourth day they saw far over the eastwards forest the upper walls of the great metallic Tower that guarded the Chilterns Dam.

They had travelled in a straighter line than the westwards crazed wanderings of Gay. Even so, hunting and fruit-gathering, they had come at no extraordinary speed. Gay had been uneasy even in the light-heartedness of those four days, and would reproach herself for that uneasiness. Nothing could have happened: most probably she would find Houghton and Lady Jane engaged in plaiting themselves fresh grass skirts – or else escaped from the Folk and on the way to London.

That London they would not believe could die! Absent-minded, her lips shaped to whistling a tune as she tramped by Rem's side:

> '*Gay go up and Gay go down:*
> *That is the way to London Town!*'

It was then that they saw the hunter. He was crossing an open glade, recognised them, waved a hunting spear in greeting. Then he came towards them at a run, and Gay recognised *him*.

It was the flirtatious hunter, Allalalaka.

In a moment, and running, he was shouting unintelligible things. But Rem appeared to find them intelligible. He halted in his tracks and stared. He began asking questions in the quick-fire agglutinative speech of the Folk. The hunter nodded, and glanced at Gay, and smiled at her, but absently. Then he sank down and resumed his tale.

Gay and Rem sat on the grass and listened, Gay

111

uncomprehendingly. Allalalaka pointed back towards the Dam, and beyond that, it seemed to Gay. He was emphatic, and gestured, and once flung out his hands in an age-old gesture of dismayed surrender. Gay found incomprehension more than she could bear.

'For goodness' sake tell me what he's saying. Else I'll burst.'

Rem turned and stared at her with remote gaze. Then, slowly, in his sing-song, hesitant English, he retold the hunter's tale.

The mad White Hunter and the Worm-Woman had been a vexation from the time of their arrival in the Dam. They had worn grasses on their bodies, as though wounded; and had induced another hunter — one who was foolish since a fall from a rock — to do the same. They had taken an overbearing part in the play of the Folk, saying they would teach them new games — forming them in companies in line, singing, and stabbing with spears. The Folk had endured this for a little, amused; then bored. Finally, they had wandered away to their customary occupations. At that the White Hunter had been angry, incomprehensibly, and had attempted to hold Allalalaka by force, and push him back into the line of those who were carrying out the foolish play with the spears. Thereon Allalalaka had taken the mad White Hunter and thrown him into the water of the Dam-lake, and that had quietened his foolishness for a time. But it did not last. He and the Worm-Woman had begun by gesture, the telling of new Songs to the Folk — evil Songs.

'What were the Songs?' asked Gay, with a sinking heart.

...They had been Songs of another day and time, the mad White Hunter had affirmed, of methods of always finding food, of grasses and ointments that would cure a wounded man as easily as food would cure him of hunger, of ways of obtaining beauty and strength such as no hunter of the Folk had ever known. The younger men and the old men and the women were indifferent, and laughed at him and the Worm-Woman: but the middle-aged men had listened, and some had believed. Them — forty of them — the mad Hunter and the Worm-Woman had led out of the Dam secretly, a week before.

'Where?'

Somewhere there (it was south-east). Next morning

112

the Old Singer had sent a company of the young men after the party; and they came upon it, and tried to reason with it. But the Folk who followed the mad man and woman (some had their children with them, and their own women) had themselves become mad through the evil songs sung to them. They marched in line at the heels of the White Hunter and the Worm-Woman; and they had plaited themselves grass-coverings like their leaders. They had cried to the young men that they were to bring back great secrets and wonders; and the young men had been undecided, and laughed, and yet were troubled, and returned to the Dam with the tale. Then Old Singer had sent Allalalaka out on the trail of Rem and Gay.

That was the story told them on the skirts of the forest. It was enough. It was dreadful, but now not so dreadful since the worst was known. Gay said, 'But what can he do — the mad White Hunter? He will only mislead the men of the Folk who have gone with him, and find nothing. All that ever was of the old days has long vanished into the ground.'

'Except the Shining Place.'

'The Shining Place?'

'It may be towards there he has led the Folk.'

Gay said, in an even voice, to guise her dismay, 'Tell me of this Shining Place.'

ii

It was London. There could be no doubt of that. London — a London still undevoured by Time and the stress of the changing millennia — or at least some portion of it. The legend of the Folk was very old and known only to the two Singers, Rem and the Ancient. Far away to the south-east stood the Shining Place, towering its airy pinnacles into the sky, a cloud-land wreathed with the passing mists. About it the earth was pitted with great holes.

It was forbidden, evil land. So the two Singers knew, and never mentioned it in their Songs. For there was no need. The minds of men were turning to other things — to those ecstasies of unnameable arts which Gay could vision only

113

dimly. In the happy Arcadia they wandered the Folk had long mislaid curiosity for the few and infrequent stumps of the past civilisation which still uprose from the ground. (No other city but the Shining Place seemed to have survived; only towards the end of their era, and as disaster overtook them, had the Hierarchs begun to build in the indestructible green-brown metal.) They had turned away, by another route, to their conquest of the stars — they, and perhaps all the dim tribes of mankind that still and elsewhere roamed the world.

The men who had gone with the mad White Hunter and had taken their women and children on the venture — how account for their lapse? How otherwise indeed than that even in Arcady there were those who still dragged ghostly fetters from the past — though they knew them not as fetters: probably saw them instead as guiding links to freedom and the full and unpained life. And on those weak souls the criminals from the past had fixed. . . .

Gay moved and sighed, sleepless, in the dark cavern of the culvert. The night-fires, banked low, burned with a smell of resin. All about, brown and naked and healthily tired, splendid of body and splendid (as she believed) of mind, slept the Folk. The faint light rayed from the tilted breasts of adolescence to the full breasts of child-suckling, the shoulders of some giant hunter — some of them were nearly seven feet in height — the head and lips of some dreamless child. They feared nothing and lived their lives, full and complete and splendid, without trappings of passion or possession. They were the children and survivors of the dreadful debacle of mankind which had nearly wrecked the planet. . . . And that diseased madness was let loose in the world again.

She turned, seeking sleep by the side of Rem; but sleep would not come. Instead, her thoughts went on and on: Was it always so, would it always be so? Some seed of desire for safety, security, to poison the minds of men and set them to climbing the bitter tracks to civilisation's bloody plateau, lit with the whirling storm-shells? That great fire that still raged in the earth near Wokingham — lit by giant bombs in the last war of the Hierarchies, or marking a spot where the Sub-Men had blown great settlements to the sky, murdering

114

themselves and their masters — there had been scores of such bombings and city assassinations. And plague and disease had come to complete the work begun in war and civil war, so that only a few scarce families survived and dwindlingly endured while the earth spun century on century and wiped the mark of that cosmic shame from its face. And then human life reached back to ancient ways, to the way of the Cro-Magnard hunter twenty thousand years before Christ, and men found happiness and delight again, and ecstasy, simple and clean. And now . . .

Was it all going to happen again? She remembered the line of an English poet, a tortured soul who lived in the times of her own generation's Great War:

> 'Look up, and swear by the green of the Spring
> That it will not happen again!'

Not happen? But what could she do? So plain the plan of Houghton and Lady Jane: they would march the hunters to the Shining Place and poke and rake in the remnants there, and find perhaps some tricks of defence or weapon-making not too complicated for their eager, starved, foolish brains to grasp. And make a community somewhere, establish themselves first priests, first kings, Children of the Sun again come to earth. And the myths and legends would rise with their lives and deaths — they might subdue and enslave all the wandering tribes of the Folk before they died — and civilisation would be launched again, with war, religion, blood sacrifice, all the dreary and terrible mummery of temple and palace and college. Kingdoms would rise again on the earth, poets sing battle again, the war-horses stamp on the face of a child, the women know rape and the men mutilation . . . all because of an accident and a chance in a night-time's dreaming at Pewsey!

> 'Look up, and swear by the green of the Spring
> That it will not happen again!'

She unclosed her eyes again, staring at the fires. She

got to her feet gently, loosening herself from the sleep-time embrace of the Singer. Then, as three weeks before, that night when Houghton and Lady Jane were tied to the pillar, she threaded her way through the sleepers and found herself at last at the entrance to the culvert, below the crumbled illegible inscription. Outside was the frosty shine of the stars.

She stood and looked up at them. No help in them. No help anywhere but what she might find in herself. *It will not happen again* — went the maddening refrain in her mind. But how? How?

She scrambled down the rocky metallic paths under the starshine-shadow of the great girders; and at the foot knelt and drank of the ice-cold water that bubbled from the side of the Dam. Far away, beyond the furthest edge of the Dam, a pack of wolves, in the flight of the hunt, with a quarry roused, were baying eerily. The sound swept nearer and then ebbed away. Gay shivered, frightened and alone and desperate. What could she do — and oh, what could she do?

Then she turned her eyes westward and saw there, bulking immensely, the great Tower of the Voices, brooding over the Dam like an evil god. It seemed to leer down at her with a foul metallic face, that creation of man's madness, outlasting him, outlasting the crumbling rock of the strata. It was *that* she must fight — that and the slaves who went to build it anew....

The stars were whitening when she came back again to the mouth of the culvert, small and very tired, but with her mind made up, and a plan, misty in detail, but firm in intention, graved on the tablets of her mind. She paused in the dimness and looked up at the illegible inscription, its dim whorling symbols of some alien shorthand.

'I'm weak enough, and so are the hunters. But *you* do not come back again. Not though we have to fill the Dam, year on year, with dust and rocks. Not though we have to tear down London with our hands. *You* are finished and past, and *men* have the world again.'

iii

All next day she talked to Rem and the Old Singer,

sitting in the shadow of the great plinths of the Dam, hearing the play of life in the culvert above them. Once there came on her again that sense of unreality as she talked with those two — *children unborn in the womb of time.* . . . She covered her face with her hands, in an agony for that sense of unreality to pass. They sat and watched her gravely. Then she took her hands from her face and smiled at them.

'So that is what we must do, if we are to save the Folk from the madness of the past.'

How much they understood of her talk she never knew — how much Rem, her lover, whose body sometimes so commingled in life with hers that they interchanged: how much the Old Singer, with that wrinkled wisdom on his brown, still face. But at the end they nodded agreement. Yes, these things would be done.

It was too late to do them that day. Gay left those two to talk to the hunters as they came back from the day's hunt, and herself sought out Liu, the girl who had tended her first night in the culvert. They had not a phrase or a word in common, but Gay was suddenly and waywardly desperate for companionship of her own gender.

'Let's go berry-picking in the woods.'

The girl understood that readily enough. She nodded, and they set out together. Climbing up from the Dam they looked back and saw the culvert distant, with a play of doll-like figures at its mouth, and the smoke blown in long banners westward, towards the Tower. Gay said, 'We don't want men with us, this once. And we've two or three hours until sunset.'

In the woods it was dim and quiet and peaceful as they gathered the blackberries in great folded leaves. In that peace Gay found again her lost self — lost on the night before, flung aside by that passionate purpose that had seized her — that purpose to prevent the return ever again to the world of the foul thing that would make of this girl — brown arm and curving breast and slim, smooth hips and happy eyes — a doll in the rags of civilisation's clothes, a thing for the dreary lust of men, not for the quick, happy mating of the caves and the forests. It was blessed just to look at her, alien though she was. . . .

Gay glanced down at herself, seeing her lighter tint

117

in comparison with that bronzed body, seeing herself shapely and comely enough, she thought, but still only one who played at the New Life.... She shook her head and that fancy away. These were her people — she was one of them!

Liu looked over her shoulder, and Gay followed her glance. Rem and Allalalaka had come seeking them. Men were unescapable.... (Not that you wanted very bitterly to escape them, Rem standing in front of you with the gleam of that smile on bearded lips and deep in amber eyes.) She said, 'You can carry the berries.'

So they loaded the two men with great leaves filled with berries, and strolled behind them down through the forest tracks. Gay and Liu had their arms around each other, and in the closing evening the silence was even deeper than when they had entered the woods. Only the tweet of a bird broke it — that and the far chirp of some cricket. Rem and his companion halted on the edge of a jagged fall of rock into the Dam — a fall of which a footpath had been made to the dull-gleaming metallic floor far below, and sat down and rested. The two girls did the same. Sideways, colourful and tremendous, the sun was setting in a wash and flare of dyes — purple and gold and dark-tinted greens, for a great driftage of nimbus clouds had come from the north-east on that wind that blew the smoke. It seemed as though a great conflagration had broken forth in the heavens.

Gay lay flat and chewed long stalks of grass, Rem's hand on her hip in that caress that still thrilled because of its very immobility. Liu was plaiting a chaplet of leaves for the head of the flirtatious hunter. Quiet and still and wonderful, lying here above the ruined Dam, in a sunset that might be the Twilight of the Gods itself, the Ragnarök of old Scandinavian myth. All around, from that sky-shining, the sky was pale and wan above the crested heads of the forests, the gleam of water in the distant north, the bushy wastes of the eastern hills. It seemed as though Time itself had stopped to hold that moment.

And then abruptly the peace was broken. The sky in the east flamed suddenly with fire. A great red beam of flame smote upward, from far beyond the bush, and seemed to crackle and break on the dome of the sky. No sound came with it, but imagination caught the hiss and bellow of the flame. Then it vanished, and with it the western sunshine vanished as well.

'Hell 'n' blast, what was that?' Gay asked.

They did not know. They had never seen its like before. They were curious, a little excited, unfrightened. The flirtatious hunter stood up, the better to survey the eastern sky. As he stood the Beam rose again.

This time it was anger. Burning, it yet rose in no wild flame, but rather as the beam of a searchlight. Its power and range seemed immense; it was as though it drove a great burning hole into the grey vault of the evening. Twice it rose and quivered, seeming to search the vault of the sky. Then it vanished and did not come again.

They went down into the Dam, hastening now because of the vanishing of the light. A diffused, violet glow seemed to hang over this lower space. Allalalaka raised his head and sniffed at the air, and on Gay also there came the curious illusion of a smell of burning, as though that beam in the east had verily fired the sky.

Ragnarök! It was no imagining she had had. For unless every appearance lied, that Beam in the east meant that Houghton and the others were already in London or its neighbourhood, reaching out greedy, incredulous, unskilled fingers amidst the terrifying instruments that survived the ruin of the Hierarchies.

iv

Thirty of them, all strong men, had volunteered for the work of which Rem and the Old Singer had told them. They were amused or mildly indifferent over the task. The Old Singer believed that this should be done, and they would do it to pleasure him — him and Rem and the gay white hunter, who had a pleasing smile. So they followed at the heels of Rem and Gay as the latter climbed in the morning light up from the Dam and took their way by the little-beaten path towards the skyey structure of the Tower of Voices.

But before they entered Gay had the hunters load

themselves with great stones, and four of them bring the bough-lopped trunk of a tree. Inside, it was dark still in spite of the growing day outside. In that faint drizzle of light Gay stood for a moment at gaze on the great machines rearing up their rods and dials into the bat-hunted platforms far in the roof. Across the floor, by the track in the dust, stood the machine of the Voice.

But what of the others? Might not some of them have secrets of power with which to contend against that happening in London? Might not they be the actual salvation of the Folk?

And then she knew that the voice of the devil, as once it would have been called in the devil-haunted centuries out of which she had come. Only by themselves, their own strength, might the Folk be saved.... She led the way through the dust to the machine of the Voices, and the naked men with the tree and stones followed behind.

Then, enjoyed as a play and an idle sport, pandemonium broke out in the Tower. The hunters hurled the great rocks they had brought into the machines again and again, till even the metal outlasting time was bent and warped. But against the great organ of the Voices the stones made no impression. Then a dozen of the hunters manned the tree-trunk, and ran back with it for a dozen paces across the dusty floor of the Tower. They spat on their hands, grinned, and gripped again. Panting, Gay and the others drew back and watched.

With a yell the hunters manning the battering-ram charged.

Twice and thrice they did so, and the great machine rocked. Strange groanings arose in it. Then, at a fourth blow that showered all the Tower with dust, Gay raised her eyes and saw the great organ pipes toppling forward slowly, ponderously. She cried in warning.

'Back!'

The hunters looked and dropped the tree and ran. All ran, Rem with Gay's wrist firm in his fingers. With a roar and a crash the great machine of the Voices fell to the floor of the Tower, and at its fall the walls shook and sang and the echo of that crash thundered across the Dam. Gay waved the hunters outside desperately.

'Quick, quick! There's something else.'

She was just beyond the doorway when the great Tower blew up.

One moment it was standing gigantic upon the lip of the morning, the next, and with a deafening explosion; it broke apart and showered the sky with its flying fragments. Great buttresses of metal were flung far out over the Dam. The very floor of the Tower was smitten up in fragments like the kicked fragments of a mosaic. Something seized Gay and twirled her about and flung her through the air, sickeningly, upon her side. As she half staggered erect another great hand was upon her, hurling her to the ground, rolling her over and over. She flung up her hands about her face, and thought 'That's the end!' and stopped with a jar that left her senseless.

v

When she recovered consciousness, the girl Liu had her head in her lap — or rather where her lap would have been had she lived in more swathed times. Gay found herself breathing in great gulps; about her was a crowd of the hunters. She raised her head from the soft pillow of Liu's thighs.

'Was any one else hurt?'

For a little while she could not discover. Then Rem pressed in through the throng. No one had been hurt but herself, though all had been flung to the ground in the force of the explosion. She herself had been the last to leave the Tower.

The Tower?

It had vanished away. Where once it had stood, seemingly eternal, was now a great hole in the ground. The power that had whispered and kept the records wound and alive in the great machine had been dying, running low, but it had still had force enough for such destruction as Gay had not reckoned on. She put up her hand to her head and found blood there. And the hand she raised was also scarred and bleeding. Bruises only, but she felt very weak and leaned back on Liu.

They carried her down to the shade of the culvert. The carrying was done by Rem, she was mistily aware, the Folk, grave-faced and wondering, trooping behind him. When

121

he laid her down, she found it was by the side of the Old Singer.

'The Voice is ended,' she heard herself gasp.

He turned bright, lizard-like eyes upon her. 'It was a mad dream. And a Gay Hunter and a Singer killed it.'

'I suppose so; and very heroic. But I wish to goodness I hadn't been such a fool as hang out on the Tower doorstep so long. I was never cut out for heroic work. Too fond of listening to songs myself, not killing them.' Suddenly, foolishly, she supposed it was because she was hurt, she found herself weeping. 'For oh, Old Singer, even that mad dream was a Song long ago, and a bit of me part of it.'

2. East

i

NEXT MORNING she awoke with only an overnight stiffness in her arm, no pain. She was late in wakening, and found Rem cooking their breakfast by a nearby fire. Liu came and smiled and sat down beside her and gestured unintelligibly towards the mouth of the culvert.

'What? My dear, I don't know a word you're saying. But you look good enough to eat. I almost wish I were a man when I see you.... (What a mess a remark like that would have landed one in, in my day! Rotten minds and habits we had!) ... What? Oh, I'll have to ask Rem.'

It was raining, that was the trouble.

No ordinary downfall, either. The wind from the north-east was driving the water in long, storm-lashed swathes across the floor of the Dam, as Gay saw from the mouth of the culvert. High in the air drenched birds were winging into the west. Condors. She turned to Rem: 'We can't set out?'

He shook a doubtful head. 'The hunters would not understand.'

'Even if they did — we'll just have to wait.'

But all that day the rain held on. Towards night it died and the wind rose to a roar, whooming through the culvert and blowing the smoke of the fires hither and thither, bringing tears to Gay's smarting eyes. She escaped out into the open, descending the path through the howl and bluster of the gale to where the rank grass grew in the sediment by the banks of the lagoon. The tufts and tussocks of grass swayed and paled and swayed again, flattened this way and that by the screaming squalls that whirled about the great Dam basin. The water lashed up against her feet. Overhead the sky was black with the racing of great clouds through which peeped a watery moon. The exhilaration of the wild cry and wheel of the storm caught her, and she cried above it, ringingly, for the joy and delight of crying, no more. To be free and naked and fenceless and herself!

But Rem in the culvert had heard the cry, even above the noise of the wind, and came down seeking her, thinking her hurt or attacked by some beast driven into the Dam in the fury of the wind.... So she gathered, leaning against him, they clung to each other in the bluster and blow and laughed, feeling the tingle of each other's bare skins, their hair tangled all about their heads as they kissed, the Shining Place and the things that might be there forgotten. Gay closed her eyes and drew down his head, and kissed him in a fashion that made him lift her from the ground in a grip that she feared would crack every bone in her body.... Fun to die that way. And then, in that moment, far east, piercing the driving storm-clouds of the sky, a beam of fire smote upwards through the night.

Rem lowered her and they stood and stared at it. Now it arced across the sky, slowly, then suddenly spun in dizzying revolution, round and round in great circles in the heavens — as a searchlight being tested and retested in the hands of one skilled but uncertain. The delight of the night vanished from Gay's mind and body. She was suddenly sober.

'Not forty hunters — we must try to get double that number to go with us when we march on London to-morrow.'

ii

Double that number.... Young hunters, mostly, and here and there a middle-aged and an aged face, the army that left the cave of the Dam next day, and held east in straggling march. The rain had passed and the wind had abated, though it still blew fresh and strong. Gay looked round the fires in the culvert, the faces and bodies of women and children grown half-familiar to her sight; and kissed Liu, and was kissed; and climbed down the path to the floor of the Dam in pursuit of the departing hunters. All the Folk crowded the ruined superstructure to watch them go. They watched in silence,

124

quiet and puzzled and friendly-eyed. Something blinded Gay's eyes a moment as she looked back.

War — armies — treks at dawn: they had known nothing of these things, would never have known of them but for a fantastic accident, a fantastic eruption into their lives of three strays from a barbarous time. And, if she and Rem could accomplish it, they would never know of these things again.

For it might not come to war — (it is damn well to be hoped it won't, for what on earth do you know about war, my girl, except that it scares you stiff, the very thought of it? Or Rem? Or these others?)...And they were marching out without any plan at all, except that somehow they must reach London and bring back the stragglers from the Folk horde, and stop for all time the clowning mischief of Houghton and his Worm-Woman.

If they could.

A desperate adventure, Gay thought, and looked back again. The Folk were lined in brown multitudes on the ledge of the Dam, no Tower behind them now. She should have said good-bye to Old Singer, she thought, as she might never see him again.

Presently the wind died to a quiet blowing and the sun came full and strong. Summer was long in this land. Somewhere about eleven o'clock they climbed up the further end of the Dam, where it sloped in shallow banks down to the floor, Gay and Rem by then treading on the heels of the easy-going, brown hunter-groups, with their spears and great dark bows. On this further side of the culvert was a speck in the distance, and eastwards, when they turned about from that last look, they saw rise before them a wild jumble of hills, bush-strewn, with woods that marched darkly down from the north.

Rem was to be guide henceforth, he who knew vaguely of the locality of the Shining Place from the songs and traditions of the Old Singer. Gay went by his side; as they took the lead it suddenly came upon her she herself was as utterly unarmed as in that first morning when she had awakened at Pewsey. She might at least have brought a spear.... Then she thought of the great Fire-Beam in the sky at night above London. As well have brought a toothpick.

125

She glanced at Rem's great spear, a six-feet ash-pole set with a broad blade of sharp, ground stone, a weapon used in the hunting of lions, he had told her. What was even it, for this venture, but a toothpick against a lion?

'You are sad.'

'Am I? I didn't mean to be. Who would be sad with you? Still love me as much as ever?'

The ghost-gleam of a smile in his amber eyes. Gay laughed. 'What a thing to talk about — two generals leading an army! For that's what we are, I suppose. Ought to be grave and earnest and important, with faces like boiled owls or constipated calves, like the militarists of old.'

'Militarists?'

'Mad people long ago.'

Mad? They had not even the dignity of madness, poor things. She remembered soldiers on the dusty roads of Mexico, with antique rifles and bloody heels; she remembered solemn processions of the Guards in Washington, men dressed like dolls, with shaven, foolish faces and inane trappings. Militarism! Karl Liebknecht had been right: it was merely a half-witted ape dressed in an old newspaper and a leaf-hat, posturing, red-posterior'd, before admiring females. . . .

Rem halted and sniffed the air. They all halted and smelled the air, Gay ineffectively. It had the freshness of the rain in it, no more. About them rose the last curvatures of the hills. Forward, the forest. A condor wheeled overhead, another followed. What was there to smell?

She asked that of Rem. He had fallen into the hunter's lope again. He said: 'Smoke.'

'A fire?'

He grunted. Then: 'You must come behind, Gay Hunter — behind us all.'

'Why?'

'Because you have no spear.'

That was sense, she supposed. Still — she peered into the sun-dazzle ahead, the sun shining and gleaming from the million pellets of water still crowning the heads of the grass. What was there to fear?

She stood aside and waited for the hunters to go by. At

126

the rear she found Allalalaka. He was pleased to have her, though even he paid but an absent attention. He had smelled that smoke.

About mid-forenoon the expedition of the Folk came on the fire.

It was smouldering to extinction. Beside it lay the hunter who had lit it. Three condors were perched on a bush at a little distance, watching him. As the expedition topped the low rise in sight of the fire, the birds rose with a languid flapping of wings. Rem went forward at a run.

The hunter had been alive when Rem reached him. By the time that Gay came up and pushed through the throng he was dead. She saw the reason for that plainly enough. All the left side of his body and face and legs was scorched a deep, angry brown. Upon this brown uprose great blue pustules. The hair had withered to whiteness on one side of his face. On that face itself was such stamp of agony as made Gay turn away her eyes.

The hunters said nothing, staring. Then Rem lowered the man's head, and stood up, his eyes very dark. A lark had broken into singing overhead, with the passing of the condors. Gay said:

'What happened to him?'

'He could not tell me. Something the mad White Hunter did at the Shining Place. This was one of those who went with the White Madman. He was burned.'

'But why?'

Rem shook his head. He had heard only a few words. Some of the hunters had refused to stay longer with the White Hunter and the Worm-Woman. The White Madman had used a fire beam....

Gay looked again, shuddering though she looked, at that dreadful death. So that was how Houghton was to maintain his empire — it was a thing like that that they were up against. She glanced round the circle of the hunters' faces — puzzled, pleasant, happy faces, neither frightened nor aware. Against what was it that she and Rem led them? What could their spears and bows do against that terror at the place where London had once been?

Rem motioned the groups forward again, himself taking

the lead. They made no attempt to bury the hunter. In the open bodies were no longer buried. Gay looked back and saw the condors returning in great flapping flight. Ugh!

iii

At noon they halted and made fires and cooked the deer killed by a hunter *en route*. While they cooked it Gay climbed a tall hill and looked into the east, where the forest uprose. But its tremendous stretch, bough-dazzling, vexed her eyes, and she could make out nothing beyond. She looked down at the somnolent hunters about the fire, waiting the cooking of their meat, and came to a resolve. They could not be led into that terror unwarned, unguarded.

She climbed down the hill.

'Rem!'

He was lying at the far end of the encampment. Gay went towards him, slowly, hesitating now that it came to the point, because, she supposed, she was frightened. Damnably. She heard herself speak in a queer voice.

'I've been thinking of our march — to the Shining Place. We can't take the hunters up there openly, until we know — whatever there is to be known. Houghton might wipe us out — he's quite capable of that, killing us all, I mean — before we ever had a glimpse of him. So you must bring on the hunters, slowly, while I go on to the Shining Place and find out what's happening there.'

'But he may kill you.'

Gay thought that likely enough, but lied into Rem's amber eyes, because he was Rem, and didn't know what lies were, and she was scared, and told lies well, being frightened.

'I'm not easy to kill. No, he'll think I've come to join him. If I *do* see him — perhaps he'll have blown himself to bits by then. I *must* go, Rem.'

He brooded on the matter, then nodded. It was her desire — how might he stay her? He would take the hunters forward slowly for — how long?

Gay had no idea, trying to think of the distance it might be to London. 'For three days — to the near edge of that forest.

128

And then wait for me there, and I'll bring back the news.'

He had stood up. 'And if you do not come back?'

'Then — oh, my dear, I don't know. I haven't thought of that. You must act as seems best to you. Don't bring the hunters near the Shining Place. Wait on the outskirts — though you have to wait three hunting seasons. And then kill the Mad Hunter and the White Worm-Woman if you can. And the other hunters who went with them as well.... I don't think it'll be safe for any of those people contaminated ever to escape out into the world again.... But perhaps I'm all wrong. I'll come back.'

She sat down. He brought her some of the deer-flesh and she ate that, a great deal of it, knowing it might be long before she ate again. The other hunters had heard by now of her intention, and Allalalaka wished to go with her. But she shook her head to that proposal. It would instantly raise Houghton's suspicions — if she ever came up with Houghton. She thought of the wide reachings of London in the day when she had known it — the wildering mazes of brick and mortar, and how impossible it would have been for a single wandering person to find another in that wilderness. So it might be even now.

'I must go alone,' she spoke the incomprehensible words to the boy, but shook her head in a negative that brought a shadow in his eyes. 'Liu would be sad if I took you and lost you. Besides, you might prove far too affectionate on our travels. Not that Rem might mind very much. I mightn't, myself. But I've years to find out about those relationships yet, and I don't want to hurry.... If I ever come back.'

At parting she borrowed a spear — one carried by the youngest hunter of the group, a boy of sixteen or so. It was light and strong and would serve her as a staff as well as a weapon. The hunters lay and watched her. The sun drowsed upon the hills. She looked round at them, this fantastic army to which she was bidding farewell.

'Good-bye, all of you. Rem...'

He came with her a little distance through the bushes towards the lour of that eastwards forest. He was very silent till she said: 'Now I must go on, for sunset will come soon.' So at that he took her in his arms, his arms under hers, his hands

129

upon her shoulder-blades, and they looked at each other slowly and earnestly, and kissed each other, and Gay gulped back her tears; and, though she had no mind for it, nodded at that unspoken request of the hunter's.... Lying beside him, she pushed back the hair from his face, and kissed him, as though he had been a child, and picked up her spear, and went on.

When she looked back half an hour later camp and hunters had vanished from sight. Near at hand rose the forest, waiting and dark and silent.

She was again completely alone.

3. The Forest is on Fire

i

IT WAS dreadful in the forest. Through the veils of the beech leaves the sun reached down hardly at all, some thick whorling of lianas interlaced the branches that met far overhead, and for a long while she walked in the dimmest twilight though the day (she knew) was still shining burnished outside. In that half-gloom her feet pressed on a humus thick and deep and soft, and once or twice she caught the gleam of regardant eyes in the dim aisles that led north and south from that main corridor she followed. It was to be hoped that food had been plentiful in the forest of late....

Then, far ahead, she saw the sun raying down on a pool of water, and in a little herself came to that pool, lost and blue in the midst of the solemn sentinelling of trees. It was circular and shallow, like a dew-pond of ancient times, and she knelt and drank by its mere, seeing herself with hair longer than it should be, spear in hand, with her brown self and her blue stare. Her lips set little ripples out in unceasing eddies as she drank.

Leaving that pool, she took to the main corridor again, and suddenly found herself questioning it. How came it that this passage ran arrow-straight through the trees when thousands of years had passed since men tended trees and planted and cared for them?

Something in the soil?

Had she had time she would have stopped, in her ancient and unquenched passion for excavation, and have dug through the detritus to examine that soil. But soon it would be sunset over the forest and, if she could, she would be beyond the confines of the trees when the dark came. She had not heard that lions roamed as far east as this, but certainly the other beasts would be abroad with the night's coming.

131

At the edge of the forest she could find a tree and shelter in that.

It grew very dark in the great corridor. And slowly a vast sigh broke upon the silence. The trees lifted their heads and listened, frozen, to that sound. Gay, frozen herself, halted and listened. Down the length of the corridor in front of her she saw the quiver of the leaves as they turned and moved and retook their old shape and stance again. She gave a little laugh. Only a breath of wind.

Presently it was more than a breath, the great gnarled trees were shivering in a stiff blow of wind, their boughs swaying and moving in a slow rhythm. Through a torn patch of the forest ceiling Gay saw the sky a moment, with great cirrus clouds going south at hastening speed. Then the movements of the tree-boughs stopped, halting, awaiting the rain.

For an hour or so Gay sheltered under a great beech, watching the steady downpour. Presently all the air was tingling with the smells it drew from bark and mould, and up and down Gay quivered a delightful chill that left her not cold at all, only with the feeling of being cleansed. Here, in this dim place of trees, watching the pelt of the rain and hearing it whip and tap on the leaves overhead, it was hard to think there was any world at all beyond these vistas. Any world at all where hunters lay in encampments or trailed down through the rains with spears, where east in the Shining Place a poor, eager fool out of an accident in time planned to bring back the filthy bestialities of old — that would shut women and men out and for ever from the clean delight of standing naked and unashamed and unfrightened under a treey canopy in the sting and glow of clean rain. Had this been England of that century out of which she came. . . .

No forest, but a bunch of trees, and the yokels of the village about her. . . . Suddenly it seemed to her that it was not only the great and towering and tremendous bestialities of that life that had been vile, war and classes, oppressions and cruelty, but the little things that had crippled life and made it a prison: the little, picturesque things that the poor souls of that time had come to cherish and love: old cottages and old ale and old couples seated in front of ivy-wreathed doors and old sweethearts and old remembrances and old loyalties

132

and old hopes. Old! What a curse they had been in her world, the old and all old things that they cherished!

She picked up her spear, and hefted it, and padded out into the sting of the rain, taking the eastwards corridor again.

Nearly an hour later she saw that darkness was not far from the land. Still there was no sign that she had come to the confines of the forest, and still the rain fell, steadily, in a steady seep from a dim sky, rivuleting warmly from her hair and shoulders. She must find some shelter against the dark.

So it was she came on the second opening in the forest.

It might have covered a space of a hundred square yards, and it gleamed, darkly, like spilt milk on a buhl table, she thought, out of a childhood memory. At first, though on the brink of it, she could make nothing of it. Then she saw it was a great sheet of metal, lonely and abandoned here in the forest, though of the same nature as that which twice before she had come on. It was a 'vision-plate' such as the Voice in the Tower had talked of — a television-plateau.

How did it come to be cleared of its covering of forest mould?

She peered round about her, but the light was too dim to see if the clearing could have been done recently. The trees grew all about the great circular plate, abruptly down to its verge. As she looked, a leaf floated past her shoulder and settled on the marled metal. She peered at it, then blinked. It had vanished. She bent down on the edge of the great disc and put her hand on it. It was cold and smooth, yet with a kind of faint quiver in it. What could that be?

The darkness was growing closer. The great plate glimmered like the surface of a lake. If she was to press on there was nothing for her but to cross it.

She was half-way across before she noted the faint humming sound from underfoot. She stopped. At that, the humming sound stopped as well. She shook herself, speaking aloud:

'Imagining things. You'll be as bad as Houghton and his half-witted female in a minute.'

At the edge of the plate, as her foot left it and sought the soft under-press of the forest-corridor again, she noted that the resumed humming had again ceased.

But now the tree-army of the English forest was blinding the last of the day. It was useless to go on, uncertain as she was of the exact direction. Better to take to a tree until morning.

She found one, a great beech, and climbed into it. The wind had resumed again, and the tree drummed and quivered against her bare skin as she ascended. Presently the wind was in her hair, lifting it gloriously from her scalp. All around, like the plash of a dark sea, the boughs of the forest swished and sang. Tired though she was, Gay felt like singing herself. Presently, in some angle or crook (for now it was too dark to see) made by the boughs and leaves, she found a spot where the wind failed and it was secure and comfortable. At least it felt that, though in the darkness it might well be that she was going to rest on a rotten branch over forking abysses. It had just to be risked.

She stretched herself out cautiously in the dry place to which the rain had not penetrated and wedged her slim hips in a crevice of boughs that felt secure. A stray waft of wind ran down her spine, tickling it. Very wanton. Goodness, how tired she was!

She had just closed her eyes, and was settling for sleep when something quivered red through her eyelids. She opened her eyes again, staring in the sky. What she saw made her sit aloft with a half-smothered gasp — smothered she did not know why.

It was the Beam again in the sky — the Beam she had twice seen before. It sprayed a deep angry red against the darkness, and, as she watched, took to its twirling revolutions again, spinning like the released shutter of a revolving lamp till Gay's eyes ached, staring at it. Then . . .

Then something quite fantastically impossible happened. *The Beam bent slowly downwards* — it bent as though seized and bent in two hands, and the angry end of it, instead of smiting into the sky, smote downwards far north. What for? What on earth was happening?

The Beam had been a red-edged, translucent pillar while it bent. Now it glowed a fiery red again and within it, miles away in the sky though it was, Gay could see the uprush of a great column of flame: it was exactly like the boiling uprush of an acid inside a test-tube. At the curve of the Beam the acid-flare seemed to split and foam. Gay's hand clutched her spear.

Far in the north a great screaming roar grew. She peered through the boughs in that direction, and as she peered saw all the northwards forest red-fringed, as though a great fire burned behind it. The crackling rose in a deafening, whistling screech, nearing and nearing.

Suddenly a far and solitary tree, silhouetted against that infernal clamour, burst as in a thunder-clap, lighting all the forest in a wan glow.

Then a nearer grove fled into rapid flames, stabbed by a giant pencil-beam of fire.

The sleep-mist vanished from Gay's eyes and she understood.

The great bent Fire-Beam was wheeling upon the forest; and the forest was on fire.

ii

Of the happenings of the next half-minute she had never but the dimmest recollection.

Somehow she reached the ground, in a reeling scramble through boughs and leaves and twigs that tore at her hair and flesh. Her feet on the forest-floor, she saw a whirling column of fire nearing and nearing, and a little hummock lying towards it, three or four yards away. She ran for the hummock, and, whistling, the Beam leapt towards her. As it did so the forest-heads vanished away, great trunks flew into flame, the detritus spouted and quivered. Then . . .

Midway a thunder-clap, lying behind the hummock, she felt it quiver. Then it showered her with earth and stones: the stones were almost red-hot. She cried out and pressed herself deeper in the mould, and suddenly her left heel went numb. For a breathless, sizzling second she knew the play of such fiery heat as no living thing might live and endure. Then it had switched away. She raised her head and watched it, wide-eyed.

It was sweeping the forest from the face of the hills. All

the countryside was now alight with a flaring earth-fire. The great trees, their trunks and boughs, had vanished away: it was the interleaving bush and grass that now flared as the Beam swung on, south. For miles the countryside was lighted in the hellish glare.

Suddenly the Beam deserted the forest — it had reached the end of the forest — and burst into a skyey geyser of earth and rocks upon the side of a hill. At that, abruptly, it vanished.

In the space of two minutes the great forest that mantled the eastern slopes of the Chilterns had been swept away, it and all that lived therein — except herself, by the chance of a miracle.

iii

All that night she lay in agony, what of her scorched heel, unable to move with the charred country still smouldering around her — in places bursting into sudden flaming maelstroms of light and fire. Thirst vexed her throat intolerably: but there was nothing for it but to tolerate it.

She dozed away at last, behind the scarred hillock, and was awakened by a roar and crackle overhead that made her believe that the Beam was returning. Instead, it was the beginning of the worst storm she had seen in this later-day England. The sky split and against the broken fragments of its bowl played a thousand spears of lightning. She thought, 'That comes of the Beam, I suppose, affecting the atmosphere. To be struck by lightning now . . . '

Suddenly she heard the moan of approaching rain.

It rained until nearly dawn. She fell into a doze, a drenched doze at last, sating therein till the edge of the morning peeped upon the sky.

The rain was fading to a thin drizzle over a churned and paddled wilderness. She rose to her feet, with drenched and aching limbs; and, in a sudden fear, looked behind her. Far away, into where the morning's soft glimmer extended, the black desolation extended unbroken.

Had even Rem and the hunters escaped?

She tried to think if any hills intervened between that camp and the far forest-fringe, whether or not the ground had sloped down to the forest or risen. Risen, she thought, but her head was aching intolerably, and no coherent thinking could be done in this plight. And oh, hell 'n' blast, however was she to escape from it?

'By walking, of course, seeing there's no aeroplane. This damned heel ... '

She was more than a little light-headed, starting; but presently the sheer physical labour of wading and scrambling in the quagmire of blackened stumps and sodden mould cleared away these vapours of the night. Her chilled and water-sodden self lit and cherished a heartening glow as she tugged and tripped and ran over gurgling stretches, and climbed down a great hog-back, still seething, like a poker in a pail; and trod up the grey, shrivelled ghosts of canyons where last night trees towered sentinel. So, after hours of labour she attained to the edge of what had been the forest.

A hundred yards beyond it, the grass rose wet and green and tall. She ran for its shelter, and, running, stumbled over the corpse of a little beast — a hare. Picking herself up, she would have turned again, panting, to that tall shelter of the grass, but for the realisation that she was desperately hungry. She turned back, retrieved the hare, it flopped soddenly and sickeningly against her warm skin — and attained the grasses at last, and fainted very thoroughly and completely.

4. A Lost God

i

SHE MUST have passed from that to sleep; she slept well into the afternoon. When she awoke a corncrake was sounding close at hand — on a long, staccato, undisturbed note to which she lay and listened uncomprehendingly a long while. Then she opened her eyes to a sky set with a slow driftage of southerning clouds which every now and then obscured the face of the sun. Around her rose the tall grass. She sat up on an elbow and pushed aside its fronds.

It had been no dream. Westwards the country looked as though a great hand, dipped in pitch, had been smeared upon it. Here and there still uprose lazy puffs of smoke, in little pools the water gleamed under the sunlight, on its nearer fringes the desolate stretch showed like a slow-moving ocean of viscid black mud. Condors, innumerable condors, were planing over the waste. There was already a sodden, putrescent smell in the air.

She moved and touched something damp and clammy, and looked down at it and saw the hare she had rescued. Its presence reminded her of an unabated hunger. It was indeed far more clamant than ever. She picked up the damp and headless body, and shuddered, being still squeamish in such matters, as she ripped off a section of flesh. It came away very easily: the hare had not only been killed in the swinging of the Beam, it had been killed, cooked, and then drenched in the thunder-burst!... What it took from her heel it gave back with the hare.

It? What on earth had caused that ghastly bending of the Beam?

Now, sitting alone, naked here in the grass, eating in a famished and unladylike manner, she realised how very uncertain she was of what lay in the east. London —

138

the Shining Place? And in there? Dimly and foggily, back in the Dam in the Chilterns, she had presumed that the Beam was being operated by Houghton and Lady Jane experimentally — some weapon or implement they had stumbled upon in their researches in the Shining Place. But could it be they?

'Then who else? There's no one else alive in England who could operate it — who would have the faintest knowledge of the mechanics necessary to operate it. Last night it must have been they who twisted it and swung the end down on the forest. But why did they do it? ... Lord!'

She paused in her eating, staring at the black desolation. So that had been why. Like using a hurricane and an eighteen-inch gun to kill a flea — but what other object was there in the wiping out of the forest? That television-plateau lying clear in the midst of the trees — when she had set foot on it she had thought it quivered in a strange way. Perhaps it was still 'working'; and Houghton in London had been apprised of her coming, had looked at her in some dim dial far off in the Shining Place, and had switched on the Beam to kill her. ...

Fantastic. But these were hours and days of fantasy. There was no other explanation. A forest had been wiped from the surface of the earth in an attempt to kill Gay Hunter.

ii

'And I feel no delight in the fact at all. Scared, if I only confessed it to myself. And what am I going to do now? Fire-Beam — when I haven't even my spear to use against it.'

The spear was back in the charred forest. Beyond that forest, for all she knew, the Beam had wiped out the expedition of the hunters. And east in London were those idiot adolescents — they'd be adolescents all their lives — playing their idiot games with the half-known tools of a brute civilisation ...

She sat a long while with her head in her hands, with a by-thought she dwelt on a moment and then let go — the thought of how much she had aged in this last month!

Years and years older than that girl who had driven the Morgan into Pewsey. Well, she had need to have aged, to be sitting here, ridiculously, with the history of humanity depending upon her. Poor humanity!

She thought, in a sudden glow of pictures, of Rem, the Singer, the Dreamer, the boy with the mist on his face, her first lover, who had shown her the deep wells of beauty and wonder in elemental human contacts, who somehow in those magic hours of the past two weeks had grown for her into the seeming of Man himself — released from the taboos and travail of civilisation, splendid and strange and sweet, so that you wanted to laugh at him, and love him, and admire him, and feel frightened of him a little as well — like a mother with a child, in fact — and cry to him, 'The world's yours — *do* have some fun!' . . . And perhaps he was no more than a charred skeleton back there in the Chilterns.

She said: 'If that's so, somehow, though it takes me all my life, I'll keep that life and settle accounts with Houghton and Lady Jane. Somehow, anyhow. I can't think and plan for all the splendid issues, I know — I'm too angry and ignorant for that. But Rem — like wiping out a fine picture of a Japanese deer to put in its place a dirty Leightonish battle daub. . . . Oh, damn it, and now I must cry about it. A lot that'll help. . . . Oh, Rem, Rem!'

After a little she said to herself: 'Idiot. Rem's still alive — I know he is. Hidden and camped with the hunters beyond the forest, and wondering how soon you'll be back. And instead of getting on with the business you're snivelling here like a thing in an Edwardian novel — being Wells-ish and save-humanitarian and oh-dear-planetish. Move, for goodness' sake!'

But rising, she found it impossible to move with any great speed till she came on a pool where she drank and then bathed her scorched heel. It had done no more than move the skin from her heel, that waft from the hellish Beam. But that had been bad enough, especially when she must needs walk barefoot. Nothing for it but to walk and endure.

So, all the rest of that afternoon, she did. In front the eastwards country wound in shallowing vales down to a point of mist and glister of which she could make

140

nothing. London? Perhaps. Why, in the classes in Mexico City, had she never paid attention to English geography? — she had thought it the dullest subject on God's earth, she remembered.

Once she crossed a great patch of grass that was not grass at all, but clover; the air grew heavy with the smell as she pressed the heads under her feet. Late bees were homing laden from that hay-field, and Gay picked a head of the clover and chewed it for the honey in it, as she had not done since she was a child. A queer feeling came upon her that she knew this place, but she could not trace the memory. And, because it was a comforting spot, she sat there and rested for a while, under the drifting shadows that the clouds flung down from the sun, watching the wheel and dance of those shadows, south into the tenebrous land she had now to tread. What lay there, she wondered? Somewhere the Great West Road, long whelmed in earth and stones and time, with all the little villages that once had slept uneasily by the side of it, in that sight and hearing of those endless auto-processionings. She remembered a Sunday she had driven the Morgan out on that Great West Road and the seething, endless snake-belt of traffic, the smell, the heat, the dust, on the great, arrow-straight road. . . . Long gone and past, with only the curlews crying there, or further west the roar and pelt of that unceasing fire by Wokingham which marked where the great bomb had fallen.

Very silent, a slumbrous hay-making afternoon. So strange and queer the minds of men! That she who had wept in a passion of remembrance for Rem should sit now and drowse, contented, a few hours later, in the quiet of an English afternoon, knowing that some foulness was plotted there in the east. But indeed, that knowledge sharpened one's eyes and hearing to the homely loveliness of the great clover-heads, the ping and start of a satiated bee. Men shall not live by bread alone.

She had a short and sweet sleep among the clover, and rose refreshed from that, and, being hungry, held north a little, seeking berries. Instead she found a great pear orchard — pears such as she had never believed grew in England, things like avocado pears, juicy and rich. She ate as many of

141

them as she could and found grass to bind up a little bundle of them. So, lightly enough laden, she came to the end of the shelving valleys and looked for a spot to spend the night.

In the quietude of the evening she found that likely spot, a great curved hollow under a little hill that would hold off the dew while she slept. She gathered grass and more of the clover and brought it into the hollow, and sat down, and ate another pear, and watched the sun upon the rim of the western country. It was still and deserted. Nothing moved there, no Beam split up through the evening. She sat and hugged her knees and dreamt over it, unafraid, cool and wise and pitiful, seeing with a strange clarity the wonder and pity and terror, not only the horror, of that strange enslavement of the human mind that had been civilisation, seeing in the quiet coming of the night not that symbol for hopelessness and doubt that so many of her kind had seen on so many stricken fields, shield-bearing in so many stricken causes. For gladness, rather. The day with its heat and fight and fear for the children of men bedevilled in the endless wars since they reared the first city, was gone. Now the Night came. Even that long day had not endured. Nothing endured.

Heraclitus, wasn't it, who had said that first, in some dreamy Ionian city with an evening closing in, more violet than this, perhaps, but much the same evening. Thousands and thousands of years ago, at the very beginning, it seemed now, of mankind's terrible adventure. And now she could look back at that saying and see the truth of it, and try to face it, as men had been so reluctant to do. Nothing endured: neither she who sat here, with the blood circling and sweet in her breasts, her thighs, her legs, her arms, her hands here about her knees, neither she nor all she hoped and believed and trusted in and was passionate for — easy to understand that neither rocks nor sun endured, but dreadful to think that one's own tiny self did not!

And yet, was it so dreadful? Death — the thing you must not face in her generation except with a flippant bluster, a quick laugh and a quick looking away. Death, so real, so quick, so inevitable, surely so unwarranted! You grew from a child to a girl, to a woman, and in your growing you grew up within you this strange, delicate instrument of judging and assessing and creating — an instrument fine and keen and lovely. . . . And presently it rusted and fell to fragments.

Nothing endures. Not though she and the hunters — or she alone, if Rem and his people were dead — were to win in this cloudy conflict down there in the mists of the east, might that fact be altered. Not though the Golden Age lived on and grew and the Folk of Rem reared great Singers and were lifted on their wings into delights of the senses and nerves beyond the imaginings of such poor crippled centuries as she herself had come from. Not though, from millennium to millennium, that simple life went on — of delight in mating and begetting and hunting, running in the cry of the wind, lying in sleep with a body that sang — thousands of years of delight, clean lust, clean love for the men and women of the world. Yet even that would not endure. Nothing endured. The very planet that was man's — somewhere in the deeps of time death awaited it, death waited on all life that ever was, the flickering of a little flame in the dark wastes of space presently to be quenched by God as a hasting hand a taper.

(Nothing endures, Gay Hunter, still and young, sport here of tremendous things and happenings; nothing endures, not even your thoughts and all the systems on which they are built. Maybe there was greater wisdom in Swinburne's vision of Death himself at last lying dead, than in that sad cosmogony of the twentieth century, which had passed on, a delusion of dread, to the sciences of the great Hierarchies. In that twentieth century the physicists and astronomers had seen in the skies the doom of men in a varying fantasy of catastrophic universes — contracting universes, expanding universes, universes that frittered away into nothingness, universes that coiled in upon themselves like — like rattlesnakes with colic. Had these imaginings had any more close approximation to reality than those of the first Nilotic kings who saw the Sun marching the paths of the heaven for no other reason than to ripen the barley crops of the Nile? Nearer to the unknown Real than the Ptolemaics? Here, in this evening quiet, you could sit and doubt even the endurance of change.)

There came the stars — the bright, cold stars, that had played so ill a game with those far imaginings of the

143

learned. For not more than a few thousand years could have passed since that twentieth Christian century — twenty thousand years at the most, the same space of time as had lain between that century and that of the ancient artists who painted the belling mammoths in the Spanish caves. And here was a sky all but alien — a sky that should have shown little or no alteration through hundreds of thousands of years! Only the planets familiar and comely against these strange, monstrous groupings in the blue-black of the sky.

She lay and looked up at them as at old friends — Venus tremulous above the sunset, the planet of lovers in the old mythologies; Jupiter, a surly, comfy glow, low in the north. She moved her gaze round the sky. The deeper glow of the stars was changing the dark blue of the early evening to a velvet black. Something else — that red glow that had companioned the evenings of her century, that glow-men in time of war had seen in the skies as the eternal symbol of War.

Mars. It was nowhere to be seen. Now that she thought of it, she remembered she had never yet seen the planet in these alien skies. It was not only the earth that had changed: the very symbols men had set in the sky had changed as well, and some catastrophe had blotted out the planet of War in the heavens, as another had blotted out the god of War on the earth.

iii

In the middle of the night she was awakened by a hideous snarling, and roused, and stared about her. There was no moon, but a great brilliance of starshine: and in that quiet glow she saw one of the strangest sights — a procession of lions, like hunting dogs, trotting past her refuge, apparently in reluctant retreat, following no trail as yet, and disagreeing violently one with other as they went. Two or three were black, great-maned beasts, like Nubian lions; whelps ran behind and Gay saw the long, sleek shapes of padding lionesses. One of these swung aside her head and growled blood-curdlingly at Gay. Curdled accordingly, she sat too frozen even to gasp, and automatically closed her eyes.

144

When she opened them again, the hunt of lions had disappeared into the softly-lighted night.

Why hadn't they attacked her? Lions — surely lions didn't hunt like that?

They were trooping west, and far enough off now. Had she known there were lions in this part of the country, she would have sought out some other refuge — a tree or some shelter blocked by a stone. But it was too late to think of that now. And apparently the lions had no fancy for her as supper. Finicky beasts....

She laid her head down and drew the sheaves of grass over her, and was again composing herself for sleep when she heard a sound seeming to come from the breast of the earth itself —*thump, thud, thump,* heavy and yet soft. Imagination?

The sound grew nearer and became more rapid. Gay raised her head again. As she did so she was aware of a sickening smell of musk in the night air. Then, swishing and leaping through the air, she saw the Horror itself.

It was furred and fanged and small-headed, of the size of a cart-horse but the shape of a kangaroo. Sometimes it leapt, sometimes scuffled forward on all fours, its short, claw-clad forepaws tearing the earth. It was a moving stench, an impossibility, a monster of starlight and imagination. It paid no heed to Gay, and, as it went by, she saw another thing: its nose to the ground, *it was hunting on the trail of the lions.*

For a little Gay lay and wished she could be sick. There could be no doubt of that ghastly shape, and the filthy smell still lingered to apprise her she had not dreamt. It had been — it was ...

It was a great sewer-rat, lion-hunting, that had come out of the eastern night — that east into which, weaponless, she planned next morning to march.

iv

The flare of the morning sunlight on her face, coupled with a ravenous hunger, drew her next from sleep. Pears, even avocado pears, had no staying power, she reflected. Then she sat up, grass-scattering. The lions, that rat ...

The countryside glimmered deserted under the early morning sun. The glare of the latter made Gay doubtful. It was too strong to last, and probably foretold rain. All the eastwards horizon was shrouded in a band of fog that moved and foamed, colourfully. Swallows were flying south, and far off, through the long grass, a bittern screamed.

She made towards that sound and its promise of water, finding a stream that gurgled and ran, hidden in the grass but for one place where it broadened into a shallow pool, reed-fringed. Here she knelt and drank and found the water sweet and icy cold. After drinking she bathed, shudderingly, and then ran in the sunlight to dry herself, but too full of thought to find much of that singing, stinging enjoyment that had once been hers in these pastimes. She was, she decided, far too hungry. . . . And beyond that hunger was the country beyond the morning mists.

There were still berries to be plucked, though here, strangely, the blackberries were meagre and sour. Nevertheless she quenched her hunger on them, and found a great root, crooked and shaped like a shepherd's staff, which she took to help her on the journey. Then she looked back over the trail where last night she had seen a great rat hunting lions, and turned her face in the direction from which that hunt had come. Birds were about their business and the sun shining. Presently out over the country went a tuneful whistle:

> 'Gay go up and Gay go down:
> That is the way to London Town!'

It had been as she imagined — the early sunlight too strong to last. Presently rain came skimming to desolate meadows, and with it — the first she had seen since that morning at Pewsey — clouds of seagulls, screaming and crying. Rain-pelted, she held steadily east, with narrowed eyes against the seep and swish of the water. So, towards noon, the rain cleared away, a sharp wind came from the east, bringing the tang and smell of the sea, and abruptly the concealing mists rolled away, leaving a sight Gay was never to forget.

5. The Ruins

i

IT ROSE gigantic in the afternoon air, perhaps five miles away, a great waste of tumbled pylons that caught the sunlight dazzlingly from cliffs and precipices of unrusting metal and flung that sheen high and blindingly into the air. At first the shapes of the great buildings seemed to move and change before her eyes, then the last of the mist rolled down into the place where the sea came, and she saw the London of the Hierarchs, as they had left it thousands of years before, when the plagues came and the Sub-Men rose.

She sat down on the little hill, breathing deeply, staring with her eyes and all her body. It looked like a vision of a dreaming Titan realised in metal and blood and tears — the tears that had gone to its building! Great escarpments of metal platforms wound like the corridors of a ziggurat pyramid high in the air where once (she thought) St. Paul's had been; and above that towering structure, dominating all the city, a great pointed pillar rose in the clouds — it rose a full mile into the clouds. Even at this distance she could see its shape and symbolism. So that was what had replaced the Cross.

The Phallus.

Leftwards rose a building like a Keltic cross — square-pillared up to an immensity of gleaming platforms that shone many-holed, as with dead eyes. Those had been the windows once, those holes, of many rooms. But the glass or other substance had long mouldered to dust. Far down, in the estuary of the Thames, a thing, squat and immense, dwarfing the temples of Egypt, but carved in like mould, bestrode the sky. Below it was a great archway — suddenly she realised its purpose. Under that arch the great ships had come sailing in the days of the Hierarchs, for still there rippled something

147

blue and grey under the indestructible metals. The Thames!

So, for a long time, she sat and looked at the Shining Place. It seemed completely deserted. But somewhere there Houghton and Lady Jane Easterling were encamped with the party of hunters they had abducted — somewhere was a building where they operated the Beam. She glanced at the sun. And she must find that building before night.

Very soberly she got to her feet and went down the hill. After a little she came on the beginnings of one of the ancient ways to the Shining City. It, like all the other remains that survived, was of metal. The grass whispered and crept over it here and there, but it still gleamed, uncovered and marled, in places. She passed the dung of some great beast as she went east. Rat's.

So it was from London the great kangaroo-like beast had come.

Drawing nearer the confines of the city, she saw it unfold more clearly, as though on a cinematographic roll before her eyes. Between the buildings that reared their strange structures, sky-piercing, were vast wastes of trees and jungle bush that crowned and covered great mounds. Here and there even the metallic structures tilted drunkenly. Once masonry must have occupied those spaces now grass-covered; and once in some day of dread, foemen of the Hierarchs had brought their unknown weapons to bear upon the London of that time. For in the north the buildings were a long-twisted swathe of ruined cables and pillars, as though a great gun had mown them down and yet could not destroy them. Against that smashed and trodden tangle she saw a great pine tree growing — she knew it great, but it looked like a fern in the shelter of a garden wall.

Now the way was clearer of grass and moss and she saw the nearer tangle of cruciform buildings rise at a distance of little over half a mile. All London seemed to watch her, as she came into it, staff in hand. Behind the towering structures that once had been hives of human activity, something winked blue and high in the air, at the top of a great, spindly pillar like a wireless mast. Then Gay saw that it was moving — a great disc that spun round slowly, like the shutters on a lighthouse lamp.

It looked about a mile away. As Gay held towards it she came on a great dead rat lying in the middle of the way — a beast that had been killed only a short time back. Some other beast, one of its fellows, perhaps, had torn out its throat. Its stench was abominable. Gay circled round it, her nose in her fingers, and went on, into a great shadow cast by the near cruciform Tower. Looking up, she saw the dizzying heights over her head like the crags of the mountains that overhung the railway stretches near Tecpan, Guatemala. Seabirds cried and wheeled high up there, and the place was thick with their droppings. Sea-birds: now the salt smell of the sea was strong in her nostrils; the sea must have come far up since ancient times.

Still the great blue disc revolved, slowly, ceaselessly, and still there was no sign of human activity. Gay put her fingers to her mouth and whistled.

The echoes rang and spun amidst the great girders. Hardly had they died away than a great rat, hiding under the foundations of a nearby building, bolted past Gay — so close as almost to sweep her from her feet. Her involuntary scream cried and cried upwards to the mile-high circlings of the seagulls. Then she heard a crashing sound in a nearby grove of giant weeds, and looked in that direction, and came to a halt.

Four of the Folk — Folk of the Dam, she knew — were coming towards her.

ii

Tied against a great metal pillar in the darkness of the Phallic Tower, she moved uneasily, and stared at the dim roof. Through it, the innumerable interstices which once had been windows and were now passages for nesting birds, a slow gleam was breaking. Star-rise. Star-rise out and above the strange wreck of a strange London. . . .

Here she could hear nothing, see nothing but dimly. After taking her here at Houghton's orders the hunters had left her for a while, and she had leant against the pillar, resting, thinking wryly that she endured no more than Houghton

149

and Lady Jane themselves had endured at the hands of the hunters back in the Dam. Then Lady Jane had come. . . .

Better not to think of that or the things she had said. Funny to think how she could have said them all the same. Unable to see her face, Gay had thought of it as even more twisted and pale than in the great hall where she had met her and Houghton. She had thought even then that both of them looked — not mad, but haunted. Haunted by some unnameable fear.

Into that strange place, a-spew and a-litter with giant machines that huddled twistingly into darkness, even though the daylight still lingered, the hunters had taken her; and so she had come on Houghton and Lady Jane, at the far end of a great room, with above them something in the roof that shoomed ceaselessly and cast whirling shadows. Before she had looked at them she had lifted her eyes to that strange sight and saw it a great revolving dial not twenty feet from the floor. It was made of some glass-like substance and as she looked at it change and revolve she saw a great stretch of the country around London change and revolve inside it. Then she had understood its purport. It was some kind of periscope.

'Hello, Miss Hunter.'

Houghton — in a grass-woven tunic and kilt, and clumsy sandals. He had half-risen from the log of wood on which he had been sitting. Gay said:

'Would you mind telling these guards of yours to take their hands off me?'

'Of course. Damned half-wits. Though they don't understand a word I say. . . . Leave her alone, you fools.'

The hunters had dropped their hands. Gay had rubbed her wrists. Well, what next? Behind Houghton had sat Lady Jane, regarding her in an amused silence. Gay nodded to her, stared at her grass skirt appraisingly, and looked round at the new stigmata of human occupancy. A fire burned in the middle of the great hall, surrounded by the shapes of enigmatic machines; further up the hall Gay had caught sight of women's faces peering from the shadows — the women of the Folk, she supposed. Billets of wood had been brought in to serve as chairs and tables for Houghton and Lady Jane. The air was a frowsy fug that caught in her throat. She had found Houghton watching her narrowly.

'You and your army seem to be making a horrid mess of the place, Major. Well, since this is civilisation, haven't you a drink to offer me?'

'I'll get you some water . . . '

'Good Lord, is that all?'

He moved impatiently. 'We've hardly begun things yet — we're just on the fringe of finding out the meaning and use of the machines in here. Not to mention those in the other buildings. . . . Sit down, won't you? I'll get them to cook you some deer.'

'Nice of you.' Gay had sat down. 'Well, and what's to happen when you *do* find out the secrets of the machines?'

'Very obtuse, Miss Hunter. We're going to put those dirty people to work, and establish a colony. . . . ' Lady Jane was surveying her critically. 'You look horridly scratched.'

Gay had nodded. 'And you horridly patched. But we always did engage in unprofitable back-chat when we encountered, didn't we?' She had looked up at Houghton. 'Why did you try to kill me with that Beam the night before last?'

There had been a short silence. Looking at them, Gay had been apprised of the queer, dull look on their faces in thought or repose — when compared with that of the face of Rem or the free Folk of the Dam. (The hunters in here look like scared savages.) Lady Jane had yawned.

'Musn't credit Ledyard with the attempt. That was my little effort.'

'I see. Just why?'

'I saw you crossing that glass plate in the forest — the reflection comes on that disc'— she pointed upwards — 'and I knew you were coming to London on some errand of those savages in the Dam. So I got the Beam working — Ledyard already had it in order — and turned a few gauges and got it to bend . . . '

'Yes, damn you, Jane. You needn't be so proud about it. . . . Look here, Miss Hunter, I'm sorry about that. I wasn't here at the time, down at the Sea-House there, searching round for any lumber left in the rooms. I ran back as fast as I could when I saw the Beam being used. Jane was out of her mind.'

'Quite in my mind. If the two of you'll excuse me, I'll go and see about supper. You might cover yourself up a little, at least while you're with us, Miss Hunter.'

She had risen up and left them. Houghton had looked after her and passed a hand across his head. Gay nodded.

'A bloody woman, as you'd say. Why bother with her, then?'

'Eh?'

'Wasn't that what you were thinking?'

He had been silent again for a while, his chin in his hands, and then, as though his voice had been released by a spring, had begun to tell her his plans.

She had sat and listened, occasionally looking back through the doorway at the waning light, and round as the fire in the centre of the hall was piled higher and the deerflesh roasted. They looked what they were, Houghton and his men, savages camped in the ruins of civilisation. What was that he said? She brought back her wandering attention:

' . . . Jane and I have married, of course — we've married without the benefit of clergy.'

'So've I,' Gay had interrupted.

'Eh?'

'One of the hunters.'

'You mean — you actually slept with one of those savages?'

'Yes, lots of times. It was very nice.'

'Those stinking beasts . . . '

Gay had looked at two of them cooking the meat. She said: 'Yes, now you mention it, they are. Filthy. But — these are not the people you and Lady Jane took away from the Dam in the Chilterns. What have you done to them?'

'Done? Nothing, except discipline them a bit.'

'I see. That's why they slouch about in that way. You've done more than discipline them — you've civilised them — you poor, idiot boy. Hell 'n' blast, *don't* you see what you're doing?'

'Shut up, damn you! I've no need to stand your impudence here, anyhow.'

'No. Savages to command — not to mention Fire-Beams. And you're going to found a colony in London on that for a basis? — when you don't understand even the composition of the power behind the Beam. It's probably a small reservoir

152

soon to peter out. It's you who are the savage — a savage in a grass kilt playing about in a museum of the twentieth century. Don't you see how impossible all this plan of yours is? Civilisation — the civilisation that built this London — is dead, and men have survived and are turning to other things — oh, there are other things, if you'd open your ears and eyes to them. And instead you come blundering into this stinking, tattered wreck of metal buildings and think you can begin half-way again with civilisation. Fire-Beams! Why didn't your mother smack you when you were young?'

'Miss Hunter, I'll have no more of that!'

'Humourless as ever.' Suddenly Gay had been serious. 'Look here, Major Houghton, I'm nothing and know nothing. But don't you see what you're trying to do — to revive a horrid and beastly thing and re-enslave men to the kind of horror that the Hierarchies built?'

'The Hierarchies?'

'Of course, you never heard of them. They left the Voices in the Tower above the Chiltern Dam.'

He had asked what Voices, and Gay had shrugged, knowing the uselessness of trying to explain. And then Lady Jane Easterling had come back, and two of the hunters had brought them some cooked deer-flesh and water. The hunters were still armed with flint spears, Gay had seen. Houghton had not been able to cast from metal yet.

Lady Jane had sat down and glanced from one to the other of them with her thin, lovely face. 'Well, Miss Hunter, what is your answer?'

'Answer to what?'

'Ledyard — haven't you told her yet?'

Houghton had moved impatiently. 'I *was* telling her —when she started some damned impudence or another that distracted me.'

In the light of the fire Gay could see Lady Jane's lips come set in a thin, even line of contempt. 'Distract you? You allow her to distract you? A little of the same treatment as we've given those savages would quieten her, I think.'

'I *won't* have more floggings.'

'Or burnings?' Gay suggested. 'We — I came upon one of your experiments in civilisation who had escaped from you here. Most of his skin had been scalded from one side of his body.'

'Blast you, do you think that was deliberate? He was the fool who first helped me with the Beam machine — a shutter fell open and he got a whiff . . .'

'Is it necessary to explain all that?' Lady Jane had inquired in her deceptively casual voice. 'Seeing that Miss Hunter escaped my attempt to put an end to her problem of being alive and disturbing the savages, we agreed to put her to a better use, didn't we?'

'Yes.' Houghton had stood up and began to walk about. Far over, beyond the glow from the fires, bats were haunting the dim shadows. There was a subdued murmur of life from further up the great building, where the stray Folk and their families were presumably encamped. What exactly had Houghton and Lady Jane done to bedevil them? They looked subdued and dirtily cruel at the same time. What was he saying?

' . . . the savages. Apparently they trust you and allow you a considerable freedom . . .'

'They allow me any freedom I want. They are the freest and finest people I have ever met.'

'Then you can help. This is what Lady Jane and I want you to do — to go back to them and persuade the entire tribe to come down to us here in London and help in founding a colony. You can make it attractive enough to them, the prospect — Good God, isn't it attractive to be dug out of the filthy life of a hunting beast and set on the road to a civilised life? And you yourself, of course, will have special privileges in the colony. Yes, she will, Jane. . . . After all, we'll be the only three white people, and if we stick together we can carry on the whole show as long as we live. A Council of Three. After us our children. You say you've found a — admirer among these — people, Miss Hunter. If you married, of course your children would have the same privileges as ours.'

'Admirer?' This had been Lady Jane. 'How interesting! And no doubt you'll soon mother him a little savage half-caste?'

For a minute Gay had bitten at her lip. Then she had said, 'I see. So that's to be the future aristocracy to rule England. Pity I'm an American with a natural hatred of aristocracies. And after we start this agricultural life, and make metals and set up houses, and get these machines in order, and ferret out their secrets, and our children control them — what then?'

'Eh? Well, they'll spread out and make a little kingdom in time, I suppose. All the old adventures. Then there's the sea, We might even get across to France in our own lifetime.'

'Better still, you could first depopulate it with the Fire-Beam.... No, let me speak now. You and Lady Jane aren't so certain as you once were that we'd stumbled into only a little accident after that night at Pewsey — you now know this is a different age and a different time and that we are probably the only civilised beings left alive?'

Houghton had sat down again. He nodded. 'And you are to raise civilisation again — with the aid of the Folk in the Chiltern Dam? Two obstacles.'

'What?'

'The first is that you're making a bad mistake if you think the whole Folk are like those forty that you and Lady Jane managed to lead away as a bodyguard. Also, they're startled and on the defensive now. You could no more get them to trek down here *en masse* and start a strange life than you would get the Fire-Beam to grow corn. They wouldn't come.'

'That's to be proved. You could persuade them. They were fond enough of you.'

'Quite. Which brings the second obstacle — that I won't persuade them, or rather, as soon as I do get back to them I'm going to raise an army of spearmen and bring them here and put an end to the whole plot. Plain? Do you think I'm going to let dirty little morons of your calibre start diseasing the world again?'

(Idiot to lose your temper....) Houghton had started to his feet, in one of his usual rages. But Lady Jane had restrained him. 'Supposing we give her the night to think it over — down in the Pillar Tower alone?'

'No. I won't have that.'

'You prefer her to get away and raise the savages against us?'

They had wrangled for a little. Gay had stood up and yawned, too tired to be frightened.

'I'd rather have the Tower any day than sit listening to your civilised domestic felicities. Where is it?'

'Then by God you can have it.' Houghton had retorted. 'Hey, you . . .' and he had called up a couple of hunters. They had seized Gay's elbows and led her out of the building on the heels of Houghton himself, into the whispering mystery of London's night. They had stumbled down grass-grown roads a while with the aid of a spluttering pitch-pine torch, till they came under the cliff of another great building. Raising her eyes as Houghton fumbled at a small side door, Gay had seen an immense pillar towering into the quietness of the evening sky. Suddenly she had realised what that pillar was — this was the Phallic Tower. . . . Then Houghton and his hunters, having led her across an immense desert waste under the arching of a cathedral-like roof, had tied her to a pillar and departed.

'You'll probably have changed your mind in the morning.' Houghton had called back. 'One of the savages was recalcitrant and we tied him where you are for the night. He was meek enough in the morning.'

To that Gay had answered nothing, sick and sorry already for the flippancies which had landed her here. Hell 'n' blast, *what* a fool of a schoolgirl she had been to twit them like that! What a damn fool! . . . The door had banged echoingly, leaving her to her disturbed thoughts.

But not for long. In less than an hour, so she had calculated, she had heard that door open, and seen a slim figure in the opening. Lady Jane . . .

Gay shuddered and moved at her pillar, tugging at the bonds of dried deerskin. But they were bound tightly and skilfully enough. Lady Jane had tested them before she had gone.

'I think they'll hold while the rats are coming. After that neither you nor we need worry.'

Gay had licked her lips. 'You won't — you can't leave the door open?'

'Won't I? Just watch.'

She had gone, and Gay had watched. Watching she had seen the doorway blind a moment and then clear again. Out of the darkness she had heard Lady Jane's last laugh — a laugh which made her shudder.

It was the laughter of a madwoman.

6. The Rats

i

THE GREAT rats, the terror of the London dark — Lady Jane had said they haunted this building at star-rise. And now the stars had risen. Looking up again, Gay was conscious of a pressing multitude of sounds, the creak of the great metal stays of the buildings, the whisp of bats' wings; but as yet no thudding noise of the coming of the beasts. A few minutes yet . . .

She licked her lips, staring in front of her in the darkness. To be torn in pieces by a rat. Best to face that squarely, now it was so imminent. Probably the pain would not last long — the beast would leap at her jugular, she thought. Or she would faint in its approach, before the tearing and slashing of those giant claws and teeth began. . . .

She was dreadfully sick a moment, and hung weakly in the bonds. Even so, her mind took up a train of thought, coolly enough. So that explained a great deal — Lady Jane was half-mad, Houghton also probably. This echoing city with its deserted buildings towering in the clouds — was that what had done it or the feeling of hopeless lostness which she herself had known — known even in the comfort and good fellowship of the Folk? Mad . . . and the rats were coming.

She heard the patter — not inside the building, she thought, but outside, on one of the great deserted ways. It flickered and flumped about the Tower, and she strained to look towards the little doorway. Abruptly that darkened.

Gay held her breath.

The stench of musk grew, while the doorway still remained black. How long, God, how long? Better scream and finish it. *No!*

Abruptly, she saw that the pale night-light streamed through the opening again. The rat had gone.

157

For how long — or how long until others came? This scene was very old, she thought, dazedly. Who was that woman in the Greek stories who had hung in chains, waiting the coming of a beast to devour her? Andromeda.

Flump, thud, flump. She closed her eyes. This time, surely. Then outside sounded the noise of a wild scuffle. A scream of pain rent the air, and echoed far up among the cliffs of masonry. Then a renewed thudding and thumping, dying away. Some fight over spoil. . . .

Noises inside the building, coming nearer. Gay braced herself back against the pillar, suddenly so pitiful for herself and the fears of her own shuddering flesh that she felt strangely serene.

Now . . .

ii

'Miss Hunter!'

She opened her eyes. Something was breathing deeply close at hand — someone. She breathed fearfully herself.

'Miss Hunter! Are you all right?'

'Is that you, Major? Did I hear you have a meeting outside?'

'Bloody rat. Was it coming in?'

'I don't know. Shame to put it off its supper, anyhow.' Her laugh, echoing up into the great metallic spaces of the roof, sounded ghastly to her own ears. In the darkness Houghton's hands came over her mouth.

'Sh! Don't make that noise.' His hands were urgent upon her. 'Where are the ropes tied? Never mind, I've a knife. Stand still.'

Something cold slipped between her bare skin and the thongs. A moment later she staggered away from the pillar and sank down in the inches-deep dust of the floor, rubbing her cramped legs and arms. Houghton's whisper was as urgent as his hands had been.

'You're all right — you can walk?'

'I think so. Where?'

'Anywhere. Get out — get out of London before morning — as far away as you can get before morning. You can

158

have this spear and you'll just have to take your chances of the rats. Hold along the main way, they hardly ever come out on it. And don't make a sound, for God's sake.'

Gay sat still in the dust, staring towards that voice in the darkness. Then she said:

'You're going to let me go free? Don't you know Lady Jane came in here and told me it was your plan to have the rats eat me?'

There was a short silence, then he said: 'Lady Jane's — not well. She's been upset. Anyhow, don't argue it now.'

She understood. He was freeing her without letting the woman know—the Worm-Woman, as the Folk called her. She stood up and stretched out her hand and in the darkness encountered Houghton's.

'Look here, come away with me.' She felt his fingers flinch and the ghost of a laugh came on her lips. 'Oh, I don't mean as my lover. Come back with me to the Folk. There's fun and a good life among them, if you'd only let yourself see it. Come back with me, before it's too late.'

'Can't. There's Lady Jane and those chaps — the savages I brought here.'

'You could bring the lot.'

'Don't damn well dictate to me. Are you going or are you not?'

Gay squeezed his hand. His fingers held hers as he guided her across to the door. In that star-rayed darkness the London of the Hierarchs looked like an infernal city limned by Doré. It was filled with the rustle and murmur of multitudinous voices — the pines under the great walls of the cruciform buildings, the whishing of the colonies of bats about their nocturnal business, the sigh of a sea-wind, salt-laden, that came up from the east. Houghton thrust the spear in her hand.

'Right straight along here, and you'll make it. I must get back, or Jane will miss me. If you meet a rat, thrust under his left paw. You've got guts enough.'

'I know the way. Look, I must tell you: if I get back to the Folk I'll still do as I said I would earlier this evening — raise them and bring an army down here against you.'

159

'Raise what you like and be damned. God, I'm sick of this nightmare! Go on, go on! . . . Eh?'

She had kissed him, suddenly, on an impulse, lest she should weep. 'Only that. Good-bye, Major Houghton.'

He called something after her, unintelligible in the dark. She half-turned round, but saw no sign of him — only the titanic shadow of the great phallic symbol and the white, marled glimmer of the way.

She turned her face towards the darkness of the west, where Jupiter burned above the Chiltern Hills.

iii

Twice she hid from rats, and once lost her direction on the grass-grown way, straying into a bewildering metallic cul-de-sac and on to the verge of a giant hole in the earth. Looking down that hole in the faint glow of the starshine she remembered the great underground railway system of antique London and the multitudinous passages and echoing caverns once crammed with a busy life. Did any of those old subterranean voyageurs ever vision a time when giant rats like kangaroos would make of the underground tunnels their runways, and squatter up slopes, set in eternal darkness, where once the creaking escalators worked? Funny how rats were in some measure always horrifying, big or little. . . .

Long before dawn she was beyond the outskirts of the great complex of buildings. Once she walked in darkness and a downfall of stinging, salt rain. Then the rain had risen, howling eerily while she trod westwards over the deserts of crumbled masonry where once Hammersmith and Chiswick had been. There was no sign of the Thames — it had long vanished to an underground bed, she supposed, like the river in Kubla Khan. Once an owl screamed piercingly as she passed a lurching edge of falling metal, and that brought her heart in her throat far more than the near encounter with the two rats. Then the rain ceased and she had seen, a faint ghostly limning of the eastern sky, that the morning would not be long delayed.

So she had taken to running — fleeing westwards through

that dawn from the dreadful city of night that had once been London — presently fleeing in a panic terror from the thing, she knew not why. Jupiter vanished in the darkness of the west, and a great star she did not know burned brightly a minute where Jupiter had been, and then also vanished. Morning was close.

Her feet trod in long, wet grass, dimness-shrouded, as she still pressed west. Presently the ground began to rise, gently, and she knew she must be nearing that hillock from which she had looked on London the previous day. Only the previous day!

She sank down at last in the wet grass, in a little hollow of the quiet hills, with the light of the dawn now full upon the earth. Lying there, she gave way at last, weeping with terror in remembrance of the dreadfulness of the night — the madness in the laugh of Lady Jane Easterling, the hopeless despair in Houghton's voice, the scuffle and whimper of the great rats in the dark corridors and alleyways of the tenebrous city. Sickening and vile and pitiful — most pitiful of all those lost hunters who had companioned the two strays on their insane adventure into London. Even if they ever came back to the Folk of the Chiltern Dam, could in some way be reclaimed, would they not come as beings diseased, to act as a fester in the body politic of the simple people who were kin to them? Sun and wind and the sight of the dawn over grasslands — pressed from that into a narrow life of filth and fear in the shadows of an insane nightmare in metal. Houghton and Lady Jane had much to pay for.

Yet — were even they to blame? They were no more than victims of their one-time environment and education and social caste; and the aberrant culture that companioned that caste in the days of its economic straits. Poor, silly, trapped beasts, trapped themselves like the hunters they had trapped. . . . And neither they nor their hunters could ever again be allowed out of London.

That grew plain to her as presently she rose from the grass and held west, with Houghton's spear trailing half-forgotten in her hand. She must do as she had threatened to Houghton she would do — either find the force that Rem had captained or raise another and lead it down on London. And then —

161

Massacre. There was nothing else could wipe clean that sore. The Folk must kill Houghton and Lady Jane and all of the hunters, men, women and children, who had gone with them, smash in whatever of the great buildings and machines were smashable, and march out of London, setting on it a taboo for anyone ever to go near the place again.

'My God, what a programme for a pacifist!'

Presently, when she looked back, the hazes of Thames-mouth had brought down their mists again to veil the great London of the Hierarchs from her eyes.

iv

She was very hungry before that day ended. She had thought at first it would be easy to decide again the route that led back to the blackened desert where once the forest had stood; but she saw in front of her, now westwards-making, a land that seemed as unfamiliar as though looked on for the first time. A jumble of grassy nullahs climbed into low hills that smoothed down to dried-up river-beds. Crickets chirped maddeningly, endlessly. The *lap-lap-lap* of peewits' wings she found exasperating, standing at this or that twist and bend of the landscape, seeking a recognisable feature. West she could make, even north-west. But somewhere between those points was the forest, and holding a degree or so north or south she might miss it in this wildered jumble, and take days to range back. It came on her with full force how easily she might miss Rem and his expedition – providing that expedition was no more than a heap of calcined ashes on the fringe of the ruined forest.

And, because this day of all days she could find no food in a country suddenly grown berryless, appleless, she met towards afternoon straying packs of dogs as hungry as herself. The first pack lay under a hillside, halted on its haunches, tongues lolling forth from slavering jaws, evidently resting disappointed from some unsuccessful pursuit. At sight of Gay the great, wolf-like brutes rose bristling to their feet, not looking at her directly, but at one another, as if

162

vaguely consultative. Then one made a step towards her, snarling, and at that Gay lost her indecision:

'Scoot!'

They scattered and fled before her rush — a flight of sheer surprise, not fear, for they gathered at a little distance, with brushes and ears cocked, watching her. A little breathless, she turned her back on them and resumed her way, the spear shaft slippery with involuntary sweat from her palms. Glancing back after a little, she saw that the brutes were following her, albeit cautiously.

That they did for a good hour or more, till a lone calf — a stray from one of the great wandering herds — uprose from a bush on the verge of a wide, green meadow. Thereat the pack wheeled from the trail of Gay and whirled across the meadow with a whirlwind unanimity blood-chilling in its silence and speed. Gay halted to stare a moment, saw the calf brought down, saw its throat ripped out, and covered her face with her hands and ran. Horrible, horrible. Yet . . .

She came on a narrow grove of great trees she did not know — poplars mated with some unknown tree, she thought, lonely and splendid against the copper tintings of the western sky. The great leafage and boughs of the trees towered high, and she climbed one of those trees to rest in safety, her nerve more than a little shaken at sight of that happening in the pasture. Yet . . .

Yet it had nothing of the horror of London and Houghton's experiments in the resurrecting of civilisation. A quick and dreadful and bloody death, and the dogs lying sated in the sun, sated with flesh that a few minutes before had made the body of a thing that lived and breathed and butted at its fellows, and grunted sleepily of nights, and mooed a foolish joy in running and sporting in the bovine way. Horrible — but rational and clean enough also, uncruel as well. Not like the Tower of the Phallus where a girl had hung waiting for the giant rat to come and devour her. . . .

'Though I feel so hungry now I'd be more liable to eat a rat than it me. Get up, my girl, you can't take roost here all the afternoon.'

Wearily, she forced herself down to the ground and through the grove of silent pseudo-poplars. Looking back, she saw them marching splendid and sentinel for long miles afterwards, lovely and unforgettable and vividly green.

In that they were contrast to other tree-clumps here and there in the long valleys up which she passed. Now she saw that everywhere the hand of autumn was on the land, and great driftings of leaves wheeled down in the little puffs of afternoon wind. She had noticed nothing of this in her eastwards travelling only a day or so before, but now it struck vividly home to her. Autumn — and coming at a speed surely greater than in the old days. (She called them 'the old days' to herself, she noted with an absent twinge of amusement. To refer to them as the days of twenty thousand years ago was impossible.)

Presently dogs came hunting her again, and again she managed to take to a tree. The beasts sat around and waited a while and yawned and scratched and looked at her with bright, pupil-less eyes, and gnawed for a while at the handle of her spear, dropped on the ground as she leapt for the tree. Gay shook the hair from her face, and considered the dogs unlovingly, if dispassionately. How long would they keep her treed here?

They gave up after a while, and trotted off, in close pack-formation, into the south. Gay descended and almost immediately thereafter came on a wide patch of clover — a great stretch of clover which she recognised instantly. It was here, three days before, where she had lain and slept with the bees about her, honey-gathering. It was here where that feeling of another-time familiarity had haunted her a moment.

Now she saw no bees; and that the heads of the clover bent, withered. Autumn. A little chill caught at her heart as she looked out and beyond the patch. Autumn, and soon the winter, and what would have happened by then?

'Nothing, except what you've planned. You'll collect Rem and go down and do that scavenging in London, and go back with him and the Folk into the North . . . '

Then she remembered the orchard of avocado pears, and abandoned speculation, seeking it out, and finding it at last. Eating pears under the great flecked leaves, the shadows waving gently upon her face, she remembered that it was close to here that she had seen the giant rat go by in the night.

She must push on west, beyond their hunting grounds, weary though she was.

She finished with the pears, and found a pool with clear water, and drank there, and tramped into the polychrome splendour of the sunset. A piling of skyey towers had gathered about that place of the sun's going down, and in the chill wind (that even up here seemed to smell in ghostly fashion of the sea) they piled themselves slowly in great structures, those towers, till it seemed a New London gathered in the skies — pylons and towers and ranging temples illuminated for a moment blood-red. Then the colour faded from them, it was only the faded English landscape at twilight, and she a lost American seeking a lost band of savages on the verge of a lost forest.

Not London. Perhaps instead it had been what Blake once saw — what was once a vision and a possibility in the days when he sang it, before man lost his vision completely:

> '*I shall not cease from mental strife,*
> *Nor shall the sword sleep in my hand,*
> *Till we have built Jerusalem*
> *In England's green and pleasant land.*'

Suddenly, far in the west, under the sunset's edge, she saw the strange star lit.

v

Presently a thin, sickle moon came up and rode the sky, shedding a faint radiance, a light like — like diffused buttermilk, she thought, stumbling sleepily. In that pale illumination the near stars burned and went out — all but the forward star low in the sky. It was the same she had seen that morning from London.

But astronomical curiosities could keep her awake no longer. In front of her, dim in the moonlight, came presently a long, wide scarring of the earth. It was the verge of the ruined forest, attained at last, but impassable at night. She sank down thankfully in the grass.

'Can't go further though it's to save the sidereal

system — and it looks pretty askew as it is. Wish there was more light to make a nest of some kind.'

She plucked grass with rebellious fingers that seemed almost on the point of fainting from her hands in weariness, gathered that grass about her, and tucked a heap under her head for a pillow. She was acquiring the habit of nest-making. She chuckled, drowsily, remembering the name hung above the door of a foolish little bungalow she had seen on the way to Wiltshire in the Morgan. It had made her writhe then. Now it was merely funny and pitiful.

It had been 'Wee Nestie.'

A leg uncovered, she bent forward to heap that with the crinkling dry grass, and so doing raised her head into the soft blow of the ground-wind of night-time. But more than that. The strange star was nearer, burning with a fiery radiance just beyond the forest, it seemed — or beyond the dark waste where the forest had been. Some celestial catastrophe?

Too weary to think it out, she laid her head down and fell instantly into a dreamless sleep, sleeping undisturbed throughout the night but waking with the first of the sunlight on her face. Waking, she sneezed violently, what of the hayseed and dust in her nostrils, and sat erect to sneeze yet again. So doing, she saw something inexplicable.

The strange western star had not gone out with the coming of the day. Instead, it was fountaining a slow pillar of smoke far away, into the sky.

Sleep vanished from her eyes as that realisation came upon her. She jumped up and sought for Houghton's spear, and heard herself singing — scraps and odds and ends of anything, though her whole body still ached with tiredness, and that skinless heel had been rubbed red anew in the marchings of the previous day.

Star? It was the glow and smoke of a distant camp-fire.

166

7. Spears

i

THE LONG flint spears glistered in the rain as the army of the Folk marched down to London.

Sights and sounds innumerable imprinting their memories on her mind, thought Gay, but never one deeper than this — the glister of spears in the spear-drive of the rain. Perhaps it came, the thrill of it, out of the past she denied, memory and thought of the multitudes of men who had marched on strange forays with shining spears.... She looked up at a sky from which summer had fled — at the whirlwind sweep of great dank clouds before a hurrying north-easter. Remote in the east great banks of fog bellied and spread under the drive of the rain.

They had crossed through the quagmires of the burned forest, scrambling and splashing amidst the pools of black mud and mud-made ash, slipping and stumbling down long corridors of calcined ash in the trail of Gay and Rem. Now they were marching south-east through the ruined pasture where she had seen the clover hang; and all about them the grass rustled and shivered under the steady pelt of the rain. Gay brushed her hair back from her forehead and turned to look at Rem, and saw his smile as he caught her gaze, and remembered that other look on his face when he saw her come stumbling from the edge of the ruined forest to the camp-fire of the hunters twelve hours before....

She had said, in his arms, 'I've come back and you — oh, you're still real. I thought that damned Beam — Oh, Rem!'

The other hunters had crowded about, patting her, laughing at her, questioning her in pantomime and incomprehensible words, Allalalaka with an arm round as much of her as Rem himself left unshielded (and that had not been much). She had looked round at their friendly faces and suddenly gone limp, happy and tired, willing and content for Rem to carry her to the camp-fire and bring her food and stare at her with the amber clouds lighting and lighting in the smokey depths of his eyes. Then she had remembered.

'Rem, I've been to the Shining Place. I know the way into it now, and we must take the hunters there — immediately.'

'It is the madness of the Voices?'

'That — and worse. When can the hunters set out?'

'When you are fed.'

She had crammed the last handful of dried deer-flesh into her mouth. Saving savagery from civilisation was certainly bad for table-manners. 'I'm fed now. Come on.'

So they had come, dismantling their camp-fire by the simple procedure of kicking apart its embers. Then they had followed Gay through the black swamp-land which the Beam had made of the great forest-stretch. At one time, slipping and falling, she had glanced down and seen that they were crossing the littered surface of the television-plateau. For a second a flash of doubt and fear had smitten her and then passed, her mind and feet busied with searching out a possible path ahead. She had found Rem's hand a help.

'Did you see the Beam the night I left you — the Fire-Beam that fired the trees?'

He told her how the thing had whistled above their encampment — they had been encamped in the lee of a hill — and swept away a copse on a distant hill, and burned into a feather of flame there awhile. He had known it was part of the madness at the Shining Place.... No, he had not feared for her. He had prevailed on the hunters to wait for five days. On the sixth day they were to march down on the Shining Place and end the madness themselves....

Gay nodded, mud-splashed. 'As we should have done at first, I suppose. But no, not all of us would have escaped the Beam in the Forest. We must hurry now, for they'll guess we are coming.'

Spears in the rain. She glanced back at their shine and something rose singing in her heart at sight of the hunters' faces, grim and kind and enduring, the tramp of naked feet and lovely bodies, east, into the fogs that shrouded

London. Dead tired though she was, she knew she could march in this fashion all night if they so willed it.

But they did not will it. The rain seeped off into a thin drizzle before sunset. They came to a drenched copse of laurel bushes and beyond that firs towered on a little eminence. Here, by the copse, the hunters camped, cutting off branches from the distant firs and erecting them as breakwinds. Then they dried great bunches of grass in front of the fires they made and spread these as beds, spreading a single bed for Rem and the Gay Hunter. Squatting under a breakwind, Gay watched the drift of the rain and toasted her toes, very near the fire, and ate the tough pemmican of the hunters. Allalalaka brought her water in a leaf, and it was while he stood over her and she raised her head from drinking, that down in the east, where the darkness was waiting, there rose again into the sky, flaring and lighting all the eastwards horizon, the Beam of Fire.

Gay dropped the leaf and leapt to her feet. The Beam was piercing upwards, fire-filled and whirling, in a long straight line through the raining drive of the nimbus clouds. But even as she looked she saw it bend and branch . . .

She was screaming and crying to the hunters as they stood and stared. Rem had gone away a little distance, but now he too had seen the Beam and came running. Gay seized his arm.

'They are turning it on us.'

He nodded, and gestured at the countryside around. The fir-tree knoll Gay could see through the raining evening haze a quarter of a mile away. Impossible to make that. From their encampment the land sloped steeply down to that series of shallow vales that debouched on London itself. There was no cover.

She raised her eyes again to that terror in the sky.

In the sky no longer. The Beam was whirling down through the rain. Northwards there sounded a sizzling crackle, and through the rain they looked and beheld the firs on the top of the distant knoll burst suddenly into flame. Then, with a hiss of snow on a fire, the long grasses caught and flamed and shuddered and went out as the Beam swept south. . . . Its glare lighted up all the countryside. Gay turned to Rem.

169

'Thanks for a lovely time. The Folk will kill that Beam yet. My dear ... '

She buried her face against him. Abruptly he shook her with iron fingers. She looked and saw a sight that suggested the sky gone mad.

The Beam had lifted from the earth, and, crooked and ragged, was whirling about the dome of the heavens in an insane dance. As it wavered and spun it changed from red and yellow to blue, to a deep violet Gay had never seen before, a violet that was somehow green. Then abruptly a great puff of darkness rushed up the Beam and devoured it, leaving nothing in the eastern sky but the cloudy onset of the night.

Through the steady drive of the rain came the chorus of the lost peewits.

ii

Twice in the night Gay awakened under the breakwind beside her sleeping hunter, seeing the soft lowe of the fires, hearing their hiss and spatter as some gust of the wind drove on them the spears of the rain. In that night there seemed no real darkness, it was as though a thick veil had been drawn over the countryside; and beyond the fire-glow the great rain-wasted meadows lifted up to peer in the camp with grassy faces.... She curled down again, and dozed for a little, and awoke, exasperatedly. *Now,* what kept her awake?

London. What would happen when they reached London? Eighty spearmen, with bows and arrows, besides their spears. To bring these against Houghton operating the Fire Beam. She visioned a belch and glow down the long ways littered with moss and the droppings of the giant rats — a flare and a puff of smoke as a charging line of hunters shrivelled to nothing — Rem's body here flaming in a second's agony and vanishing into ash. Hopeless attempt!

She put her arm around the sleeper, in a desperate gesture of protection, and he turned round and held her, and that was comforting. She saw his sleeping face dimly, and put up a hand to wipe back the blown hair from his forehead. She felt towards him an odd tenderness again — not of the lover, but for one immeasurably dear and immeasurably younger than herself. Her hand brushing through his hair sent it crackling with a faint fire. Even his hair was alive and vibrant. ... So for a little she lay in an idle tenderness, and then again that sickening depression touched her, so that she drew away from the warm contact of his legs and chest, and crouched by herself a moment in the shelter of the breakwind. The near fire was dying and she heaped it afresh with the rubbish from the firs — cones that spat and spluttered and kindled smokily, handfuls of twigs from the boughs they had used in making the breakwinds. Leaning out to the fire the wind blew on her hand and puffed wetly up her arm. She stood up and looked around and the rain fell softly in her face.

All the countryside slept, wan and dim, and silent, but for that unending wail of peewits. The fire kindled by the Beam in the north had long been extinguished. Westwards, through the drive of the clouds, an occasional star showed and then closed from sight as a fresh whisper of the rain came murmuring across the sodden grass. Around, behind their breakwinds grouped in a shallow half-moon in front of the fires, the hunters slept soundlessly, unguarded, uncold, unfrightened. All but herself.

And once again that feeling of unreality descended upon her — stiflingly, for an instant, so that she gasped with wrenched lungs and panting lips, so that before her eyes the scene flickered and faded and she felt herself hurtling down an abyss of dark terrors. Rem!

The thought of him steadied her. What on earth caused that odd faintness? Unreal? — these, the realest and lealest and truest folk she had ever known? Real and splendid, all of humankind that had survived the filthy night of long ago. . . .

The human drift! She remembered a book with that title she had once read, a book that foretold strange worlds and lives in the future, and forgot (as all those books had forgotten) that not even in the sunshine does humankind drift. Always and eternally (she thought, the rain in her face, her eyes half-closed as she looked at the sleepers) we march. Even these Folk in this second Golden Age — they were out on an Expedition terrible and strange, into the wastes of time

171

and space, on that conquest of the universe Men may not deny.

The sleeping expedition! She thought if she could make songs and sing them, she would surely do so now, in this storming autumnal night while the army of the hunters lay around her, and an unguessable morning was hastening up from that darkened east. Sing: sing the glory of the human spirit and the human body, unconquered and tremendous and lovely, lovely in its passion and pity, sing . . .

> 'We mix from many lands,
> We march from very far,
> In hearts and lips and hands.
> Our staffs and weapons are
> The light we walk in darkens
> Sun and moon and star.'

The rain ceased to blow on her face, lifted by the wind and hurled sleeting over the dark Middlesex lands.

> 'Out under moon and stars
> And shafts of the urgent sun,
> Whose face on prison-bars
> And mountain-tops is one,
> Our march is never ending
> Till Time's march be done.'

After all, what though they died in London? They would not die alone. Houghton and Lady Jane would go with them — though the last of them had to crawl a half-cindered corpse to shove a spear into the pitiful fools. And there were other Expeditions. Always. Man did not die. Even civilisation had failed to kill him. Men died, but Man lived, a child as yet, but immortal and terrible in the eyes and hands he lifted to the skies. The fevers of religion and science and civilisation had passed away, and out again, in the wastes of Time, spear in hand, he stumbled on a quest undying, with rain in his face and the wail of peewits to companion that endless trek. . . .

She sank down again beside Rem, with wet face and hair and a drowsy content in her heart.

The rain whispered eastwards in the night.

The wolf woke her, licking her face. It was barely daylight, and only a few of the hunters, yawning, were as yet on their feet, their brown bodies glistening. All about was fog as fine and thick as carded wool —it was impossible to see more than a few yards beyond the encampment. The rain had ceased, and overhead the sky was breaking a powdered pearl. Gay coughed in the fog, and pushed aside the wolf, and shook Rem awake.

'Time we marched again. Sleepy?'

He had come instantly awake, as always. And, also as always, he made no reply to a question which did not need it. He stood up and found his spear and went and scattered the near fire. Gay sought for her own spear, yawning.

They filed away into the westwards mist, Gay and Allalalaka in the lead. It clung about their faces and shoulders like cobwebs, soft and slimy, and under that soft blanket no whisper of a sound came to their ears. But all the eastwards world was afloat with a pale dun colour, and under that colour lay London. Gay knew that a direct march of an hour would bring them within a few miles of the Shining Place, and suddenly she realised the benison of this fog. They would creep into London unobserved in the great periscope.

At that thought she sent back word for Rem to come up, and whispered her plan to him. The fog seemed to call for whispering. He nodded and said something to Allalalaka, and then fell back, calling to the other hunters. Presently their pace had increased to a long, loping trot. Steadily the radiance in the east grew deeper in colour, changing from faint yellow to a dun red. The fog was thinning.

Worse than that, Gay, running, now felt on her skin the soft stir of the wind. Slowly the mist-veils about their progress thinned. The hunters' lope slowed down as they came to the crest of a hill, and a sudden premonition of disaster awaiting them touched Gay.

'Rem! We can't go further. The mist'll have cleared in a minute and we'll be seen.'

The expedition came to a halt and spread out and squatted

on the dripping grass. Rem and Gay stood erect, staring into the lightening east. Now it was possible to see far down the hill into the moving shroud that covered the ruined city. Gay whispered again:

'We must make the hunters hide here all through the day and then creep down on the Shining Place at night.'

He nodded, and went calling softly among his fellows. When he had finished with that, he came back and sat down. Gay still stood. He put up his hand on her leg in the old, remembered caress, and she drew her eyes from that peering into the east, to look down at him. . . . And again that sickening feeling of unreality caught her.

She sat down, shaking. The grass was damp and soggy. She leant against him, albeit her eyes would not leave the east.

'Yes, please. This is an invitation for you to cuddle me. Tight as that.' In the security of his touch she lay for a little against him, silent. His young, bearded face looked down on hers. She said: 'Your heart has a nice, even thump . . . I'm all nerves. Don't bother to understand. Hadn't the Folk better lie flat in the grass?'

'When the mist has cleared.'

It was unveiling as though Middlesex were lifting ensaffroned fingers to undrape her face. A sweet and lovely and desolate face, Gay thought. A bird cheeped damply somewhere in the grass. The wind shook the wet hay on the hill-brow, gently, so that through the silence of the morning one heard the fall of the spilled drops of water from the grass-heads. Suddenly the wind veered and Gay's small nostrils quivered in the smell of the sea. And there, five miles or so away, the giant pillars and pylons of London came marching tremendous out of the haze.

A low cry and murmur came from the hunters. None of them had ever seen it before. Bestriding the sunrise rode the giant Sea-House with the water lapping below it, its thousand storeys gaping windowless westwards. Nearer rose the Tower of the Phallus, the great symbol of shame and sterility pointing its rounded end high in the sky — it towered a mile into the clouds of the hasting autumn morning. Pylons and towers, a gleaming city as the mist unrolled its banners from dizzying ledges a half-mile above the ground and wreathed down from terrible crags to the sweep and long flight of giant buttresses thundering into the dawn. Gay's heart came into her mouth.

Lovely, fantastic and terrible London! Twenty thousand years since she had looked back on it from that hired Morgan, in the cottage by Pinner. Pinner! Suddenly it came on her why that hay-field with the clover had seemed so familiar. Oh God, it couldn't be, and yet — that was the hayfield behind Nurse Geddes' cottage!

Twenty thousand years — and it had survived unchanged by chance or time. Nurse Geddes and her sharp, bright face and voice and — oh, those biscuits she had made and fed to a girl long ago — a girl called Gay Hunter, not *the Gay Hunter*, a girl who had had a pleasant wit and a flippant manner and multitudes of dreams. . . . She opened her eyes and blinked something from the eyelashes. The mist-webs, damn them.

Suddenly she sneezed, violently, tremendously, so that even Rem started. And it was in the moment of her sneezing that above the distant cruciform building there awoke a strange glow.

It was as though a pale-blue fire had been kindled within it, and poured out its unburning flame from every crack and cranny of the giant structure. The whisperings and murmurs among the hunters died away. All had seen it, suddenly springing to being. The blue altered and became a glaring, still slash of colour in the heart of London. It tore at the eyes. Gay put up her hands to shield her face. The air was deathly still.

And then the earth shook, like a frightened horse, and then went mad. It bucked and clawed and heaved. Gay's hands fell from her eyes to clutch at the ground and in that instant, as once with the Cities of the Plain, God smote on the Shining Place.

iv

By noon that day Rem and Gay had succeeded in gathering together the surviving hunters, fifty-three in all. The rest lay mangled to pulp under the raining fire and brimstone boulders which spewed from the earth, in the place where

175

London had been, and bombarded the countryside around as with an enormous fall of meteors. And in that place where the Shining Place had risen a great waste volcanic stretch flamed and spat in spume as the boiling waters of the sea poured in.

8. Sing for Me

i

WITH THE coming of the morning a kind of faint milkiness formed in the tops of the trees — not light, but neither was it the lower darkness that shrouded the sleeping earth. Turning in sleep, Gay saw that light and felt the morning chill that came with it, and relapsed into sleep again. When next she turned and sought a more restful position it was with the blaze of the sunshine on her face.

Rain and cloud had cleared away. The hunters were yawning and stretching cramped legs and peering around them in a day that might have been the beginning of a summer. Rem was missing and Gay set out in search of him, drawn by the sound of splashings beyond the copse where they had slept. She came on him standing upright in the midst of a miniature stream laving himself with water so that he rippled and shone as though his flesh were made of brown quicksilver. Flinging back his hair from his face, he saw her and waved. Shivering Gay tip-toed into the water beside him.

'Splash me as well.'

He did so, generously, while she wriggled and protested and then was moved, what with the coldness, to a frenzied retaliation. They were cascading the water upon each other when the other hunters came trooping down to join in the fun. There seemed a unanimous agreement that Gay ought to be splashed. She ran from them at last, and climbed the hillside to sit there and dry in the sun and wind, looking down at the horse-play in the stream.

Dripping and grinning, some of the hunters went back to the camp for their bows and vanished across the pastures in search of breakfast. Rem came striding up to sit beside Gay. She made room for him on a thick tussock of grass, and went on with the task of wringing out her hair and then combing it with her fingers into the drying maw of the sun. Remote and far off in some morning-touched tangle of jungle, a cock began to crow.

In the east, against the sunrise, the sky was tipped with smoky torches.

'Rem — we've finished with all that! Can you realise it? I can't yet — quite. Finished with that horror that darkened our lives from the Shining Place — we need never lose each other for a day again! . . . Need we?'

He also was looking at that far torch-glow that had been London. 'Not until we go hunting again.'

'We'll do it together in future . . .' Suddenly, in the morning of clarity, she saw life unfolding page on page of pictures for her delight — far and far into the future, into old age. She saw herself with the hunters marching back to the Dam in the Chilterns, to the welcome of the Folk, the kiss of Liu, to days of play and laughter and good fellowship as the autumn stretched to winter. Then into the North with the migrating Folk, on the heels of the great herds, into days and suns innumerable, Rem beside her, Rem to teach her his songs, to help her grope a way up that dim stair of understanding and new knowledge the Folk were mounting. Winter in a cave, the roar of a fire within, the roar of storms without, no clothes or furnishings to bedevil life or hide the stark, fierce face of things. Life like a song, terrible and true, stark as themselves. Children — children like brown naked flames, singers and hunters. . . . She turned to Rem and saw him a misty outline beside her. Her heart came in her mouth as she groped for his hand.

' . . . these idiotic fits! Faint for food, I suppose. Pull me up, like a dear.'

The hunters brought back pears and pig-flesh, and they cooked the latter, and drowsed through breakfast, and then put out the fires and set out on an unhasting trek back to the Chiltern Dam.

All that day the expedition straggled miles to right and left of the central march of Gay and Rem, hunting berries, hunting deer, odd hunters lying down for short naps in the sun, hunters wandering in singing groups, hunters merging in and out of the brown gold of the autumnal landscape as though part of the play of sun and shadow themselves. (And out of the earth and sky.) Knowledge of that kinship entered your heart and you walked the ways of the wind and the ways of the sun of no volition of your own at all, but the volition of all life that was, that moved to being in grass and tree and the flicker of a bright bird's wing. A kind of Indian Summer had touched all the countryside; the bees had come back. Never-seen, the *lap-lap-lap* of the peewits sounded over distant meadows. And again, this time as they sat and ate dinner under the shade of poplars by a deep, brown pool, Gay heard the far crowing of the jungle-cocks.... The sound vexed her to a moment's unreasonable, foolish fear.

So, sun-tired, late in the afternoon, they breasted a crest and Gay cried out in recognition of the place — the hayfield where long ago she had lain in sleep and rest that time she pushed down to the Shining Place as a spy; where, long before that, dimly now she remembered, she had sat at tea with Nurse Geddes' comfortable bulk beside her. She called to Rem, 'Can we camp here for the night?'

'If the others will.'

They stood and hallooed the others, and these straggled in in hazy groups. Here was as good a place as any. In a little there rose the reek of wood smoke in the air and the equal reek of torn flesh being hacked for cooking. Gay lay on her back and smelt them both, and hated neither, beyond hate or love, as the little German poet-man had said — though he said it of other things, she remembered: horrific humans he *had* dreamt, poor, whiskered soul in a waistcoat and thick Teutonic pants! What dreams men had dreamt of past and future in the flicker of the brief dreams that were their own lives!

The hunters dreamt seldom or ever. They were without inhibitions or complexes or all the rest of the sad, futile fantasies civilisation and Sigmund Freud had once foisted on men. They did not dream of life — they lived it and sang it instead.

She called to Rem and he came and sat beside her, with that absent caress, with the lights coming lit in the amber depths of his eyes. (Sometimes those eyes frightened you a bit, like a fool — seeing they could light for you so! But remote —

so chillingly remote on heights of thought your feet had never found.)

And suddenly, though she had said nothing, he seemed, for the first time, to understand. She was to remember that when all else had grown dim, that sudden speech and look — as though mankind had looked back a compassionate moment before it turned from the shadows to the daylight:

'There are many Songs — this we live, and that which you lived. And all are part . . .' he hesitated in his soft sing-song, and sought for words in that alien tongue of the Voices — 'of a greater singing. Even though it may not be with us, you have still your own Song.'

'Not with you? Rem — what do you mean?'

He shook his head, hair and beard blown softly in the wind. It was near twilight again. All along the verge of the western sky England slept ruined, and desolate, and free. A stag was belling, tremendously, far in the north. A murmur of laughter came from a group of hunters about a fire. For a moment a frozen fear took Gay. She said, desolately, 'Oh, Rem, all this has just been an adventure and a play until now! But — there are other things . . . All lives and times Songs in the mind of a Great Singer, none real, none unreal, none but is somewhere sung. . . . Sing for me, Rem.'

ii

She saw a distant hunter, against the sunset, sitting in almost the position she herself sat in, hands clasped around his knees. Sitting and lying, the hunters listened: in the sweep and fall of the shadows Gay saw herself in her listening companioned by a multitude. The fires flickered and blew and sent their long writings of smoke up into a sky that drowsed from dull azure slowly into a velvet black.

And Rem stood singing.

At first, in the first slow chords of his singing, Gay had sat and listened with that feeling of lostness, of an alien, still upon her. Then the warmth of his voice warmed her, drew her up beside him where he stood and sang. He sang not now of sleep and love and lust and the mating of bird and beast as once before, long before, he had sung in the Vale of the White Horse. He sang now of birth, she thought, and the coming of the birds in Spring, and winds in the boughs of the apple-trees and the stars at night in the apple-blossom. He sang of the Spring of a World that had forgotten winter, yet where winters came and passed unceasingly, unendingly, amidst the lives of men. He sang of the vigour and the madness of youth, the deep days of silence that companioned manhood, the coming at last of old age and rest: these, the mere background for the essence of his Song. For he sang of Life as a fine bright fire, tremulous, tremendous, against the dead wastes —Life and its splendour in the touch of hands, in the touch of lips and bodies and words, in its pain, in its pleasure, its tiredness, its madness. Living himself, he sang the Pæan of all life, a naked savage in a ruined pasture beyond the wreck of man's greatest dreams....

And Gay saw the sunset wheel down over them and over that ruined England that knew not its ruin, over dreams mislaid as a sleeper at morning mislays the fantasies of night. The dusk came striding up the waving grasses in bands of a flickering blue that changed to black, black raiders against the grey-green monotone of daylight. Under the throbbing chords of the Song rose no other sounds, no twitter of birds, as the Singer faced the Night....

Then again over Gay there swept a great desolate fear. She tried to cry out to Rem, and could not, and covered her eyes. And in that moment, far away on the verge of darkness, as the strange world in the pits of Time faded from her sight, she heard a drowsy crowing of cocks.

9. The Return

i

'THERE NOW, I knew there was nothing much wrong with you, bless you, though you've been sobbing and shivering all night that way. Such carryings-on!'

Sheets. A window. A window-curtain flapping against a grey light. And — oh, most impossible of all — the face of Nurse Geddes. Gay gave a moan.

'Nurse! What's happened? How did I come to be here?'

'Carried you in myself, of course. How you got out there in the meadow I *can't* imagine. All this nudist nonsense — Gay, I'd 'a' thought you'd 'a' had more sense. Browned like one of them horrid little Mexicans — scratched and worse. Don't know why, either, I surely smacked you well enough in the old days.'

Gay sat up, dizzily. 'Listen, Nurse, *where* did you find me?'

'Why, Gracious Goodness, haven't I been telling you? Out in the paddock there, among the clover, about ten last night when I went on a stroll before going to bed. There you were, lying stiff and stark — nearly lost my supper looking at you. Then I says, "Well, it's Miss Gay — damn if it isn't, and them folk at the Pewsey hotel writing about her leaving her luggage and clothes in her room and her bill not paid. H'm — left her clothes all right ..." So I picked you up and brought you in here.'

'For God's sake, open that window!'

'But, lovey, it's raining. There, there, you're still light-headed. I'll make you some gruel and you can tell me where you've been this last six weeks ...'

'Six weeks?' Gay lay down again and closed her eyes. 'Six weeks. ... Oh, Nurse, Nurse!'

Nurse Geddes was cuddling her, fiercely, protectively. 'There, there, don't tell me if you can't! Don't worry your dear

182

head about it, Miss Gay. You can go and do what you like, though I *do* wish you'd at least wear them hikers' shorts.'

'What, twenty thousand years away? ... I've been twenty thousand years away in the future, Nurse, and I was sitting in a meadow the last of it, the Folk round about, and Rem was singing ...'

'Well, well, the carryings-on they *do* go in for. I never did hold with them funny trips. You lie still now, lovey, and I'll bring you some ...'

'Nurse!' Gay sat up, still dazed, but slowly awakening, in the lovely unaccustomed luxury of sheets. 'I'm not mad, and I'm not ill, but I've been twenty thousand years away. And I haven't come back for gruel. Tell me: Is there still some coffee left in the world?'

ii

There was coffee. There was a cigarette. There was the blessedness of clean sheets. There was the beatitude of stepping out of bed and placing one's feet on a soft and furry rug, and standing and staring at oneself, unforeshortened, un-caricatured, in a full-length mirror. Staring in wonder at someone inches taller than that night at Pewsey, taller, with thinner cheeks and hips, and blue eyes not Gay Hunter's ...

Where were the hunters now? Now? This was the now! The folk — Rem — Wolf — the Chiltern Dam — the Forest of Dreadful Night, the London of the Hierarchs — they were fading like a dream though she dropped her cigarette and dropped on her knees in a passion of desolation and reached after them, sobbing.... and all around, impossible as them, a twentieth-century morning was breaking.

Real — this or they? And then she remembered Rem's words: that there were many Songs — Songs thick as leaves on an autumn gale, all of them real, all unreal.

'Oh, Singer, Singer, but I never thought you'd be missing from any one I sang!'

Outside she heard the drowsy cheep of wakening birds. She crept to the window and stared out at that strange day coming on an England that was the living England of her own life-time. A motor-lorry purred up a distant road. Very far off, its voice muted in distance, a train hooted under some tunnel. The sky was barred with red. Down in the kitchen, breakfast-making, she heard Nurse Geddes. Back — she was back again and her own world wakening again....

Houghton and Lady Jane — somewhere, somehow, had they come back as well?

And then, far down in the east, across the roofs and pastures of Middlesex, she saw the glow of London under the eastern sky. London — London there yet, alive, with its teeming streets where no great rats hunted the black lions or ruins towered roofless to heaven — where still men lived and hoped and dreamed — might yet, as in all the world, build them a life that would never know the nightmare of the Hierarchs. London: and beyond it the Atlantic, its ships, New York, all the days that would yet be hers who had dreamed a dream to give her a guerdon for life. Frightened? Afraid? Hopeless? When there were still pity and kindliness in her world, humour and love and irony?

Nurse Geddes heard her whistling as she sought unaccustomed clothes. Like a starling.

That was better.

She loaded a tray and puffed genially upstairs.

There are many Songs.